A PLACE IN THE STORY

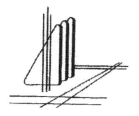

A PLACE IN THE STORY

Indebted to the Past,
We Owe More to the Future

Don C. Davis, ThB, BA, MDiv

Archway Publishing books may be ordered through booksellers or by contacting:

Archway Publishing
1663 Liberty Drive
Bloomington, IN 47403
www.archwaypublishing.com
1-(888)-242-5904

Cover inspiration by Nolan Davis

ISBN: 978-1-4808-1531-5 (e)
ISBN: 978-1-4808-1532-2 (sc)
ISBN: 978-1-4808-1530-8 (hc)

Library of Congress Control Number: 2015901611

Print information available on the last page.

Archway Publishing rev. date: 3/10/2015

ACKNOWLEDGEMENTS

A Place in the Story is the best of positive future-vision fiction, inspired by successful achievers.

Inspiration for my novel in seven sequels, *A Place in the Story*, has come from multiple sources, but none greater than from my wife, Mary, and our sons, Charles and Nolan, and their families. Mary, whose own success story continues to inspire her family, has been my devoted supporter and skillful editor. Along with these, there is the continuing influence of having loving parents who were good people.

The overview nature of my books has come from a list of writers whose books and articles explored the future, advanced knowledge, shared their knowledge base from science and technology, inspired positive insights, and led the way to a knowledge-based faith.

Those who have had a major influence on my thoughts and paradigms include: Norman Vincent Peale, Napoleon Hill, Albert Schweitzer, Og Mandino, Carl Sagan, Norman Cousins, Bill Gates, Fulton Oursler, Dale Carnegie, Theodore Gray, Norman Doidge, Martin E. P. Seligman, Michio Kaku, and others, whose vision is a reference to the future more than to the past.

From these, I have gathered an overarching view of the future. Like an impressionist painting, these provide a bigger picture of our place in the story for new tomorrows and the new sacred.

From: Drew Carvelle *drew/cassie@crx.com*

To: Dr. James Kelly *james/maria@crx.com*

Dear Dr. Kelly:

I am writing on behalf of several people here at Center Church, especially Dewey Campbell, whom you know, Dr. Ray Hart, our program director, and several others who want me to extend a special invitation to you. As minister here, I heartily join them in this invitation.

We are pleased that you have chosen to be at the last five of our Kindness Breakfast Bazaars. You have become a celebrated guest at these events and many of the people here have read your books. We have learned that you are nearing completion of a new book as a sequel to your books, New Tomorrows, Apple Blossom Time, and The Future We Ask For.

With great interest in your newest book, we are all hoping you will be willing to come to our church and give a series of presentations about the new book. We would welcome as many sessions as you would be willing to give, perhaps a series of four evening sessions.

We know this is a bold request, but sincerely hope you will be able to honor it by sharing your ideas with us. We have an endowment, but that doesn't provide us with great resources out of which fully to pay you, so your coming would be an act of extended generosity, along with what compensation we could give.

If this is of interest to you, we would like to have you as our guest at lunch soon to explore the possibility of such a special event.

I look forward to your call or email with a positive response to what would be a great privilege for all of us. Phone. 401-921-8008

Cordially,

Drew Carvelle

From: James Kelly *james/maria@crx.com*

To: Drew Carvelle *drew/cassie@crx.com*

Dear Rev. Carvelle:

I gladly accept your gracious invitation. No pay is needed, or desired. I would just be honored to come. While I am usually given compensation when I speak, it is never a fee I charge - just what they choose to give. But in your case, I do not want any compensation at all, and choose not to accept any. Just the privilege of having an audience in your very special church would be more than enough!

I do think it would be good for us to meet to talk before we finalize plans. My ideas are not without some controversy. They are not proven ideas, but then, leading-edge ideas are not expected to be proven - just explored and tried. My venture ideas are in the nature of inquiry and search for paradigms of the new sacred in the digital-molecular-information age.

I would welcome such an opportunity to have an interactive audience for my new book and would welcome feedback. That would be important to me, but I hope such a time of sharing ideas would be of mutual benefit.

I would be pleased to share lunch together with those who choose to meet. Needless to say, by my having been at the last five of your Kindness Breakfast Bazaars, I am impressed with you and your people, and look forward to this time of sharing.

Call me so we can plan a time and place to meet to converge our plans. My cell phone number is (401) 921-4404.

Cordially,

James Kelly

CHAPTER ONE

A Call From the Future

Kindness ought to be the leading identity marker
for a church's mission to its community.

SUNSET LEFT LONG, SOFT SHADOWS ON THE WHITE, WEATHERBOARD, rural church on the hillside as people gathered to hear Dr. James Kelly talk about his latest book, still in process. Inside Center Church's large conference-dining room, a large gathering waited eagerly as Dewey Campbell, country gentleman and longtime member of Center Church, walked up to a single pedestal lectern on the platform. His broad smile was framed by a suntanned face and wavy graying hair. Gradually the chatter of voices, already muffled by the plush carpet on the floor and flowing draperies on the windows, subsided to a hushed murmur, then grew quiet with expectation.

"Good evening, and welcome!" Dewey said simply. "Ordinarily, you would expect our very personable and much loved, young minister, Drew, to open this session. And that is what I expected, until he simply insisted that I do this. He insisted, saying it was because I was the first one to talk to Dr. Kelly when he showed up here at our Kindness Breakfast Bazaar five years ago. But, it's

1

more a part of our minister's leadership style. Reverend Carville says he didn't come here to be "the" leader, but to be on a team of leaders. He claims I was the one who had started the idea for that special breakfast, and maybe I did help, but it really grew out of our minister's concept that kindness ought to be the leading identity marker for a church's mission to its community.

Since that Saturday morning, when I first met Dr. Kelly, I, and many others here, have read his books and learned that kindness is also central in his thinking and writing. One of the ways Dr. Kelly lives out his focus on kindness is by his positive response to our invitation to come to our church to talk about his latest book, in process. His concepts are leading-edge and future oriented. I welcome that. I should say, "we" welcome that, since so many others have been a part of inviting Dr. Kelly to come here. In recent years, this church has expanded its conference facilities and ministries as a special place to present paradigms which help us to make our faith, not only current with the times in which we live, but a working faith that is open-ended and growing with the times.

Paradigm is not a word we usually use while we are out baling hay, or doing home and family activities, but it's a word Dr. Kelly uses in his books to indicate the changes which call for us to look at things in new ways. Once someone asked, "Do you know what a paradigm is?" A quick reply came. "Yep. Sure do. It's two dimes together." As a credit to this church, all of us know about paradigms and new ways of seeing things, which makes this a special church that all of us are privileged to be a part of. So, I represent all of us in extending our greetings and enthusiastic welcome to our very special guest this evening. He is a distinguished and respected retired minister. He is also a writer, professor, philosopher, and noted speaker. And beyond that, he is one of the kindest and most congenial persons any of us will ever meet. Many of us have read his books. He has graciously come to share in what he says is to be a dialogue of ideas as he completes his next book. So we welcome, and I now present, Dr. James Kelly!"

An enthusiastic applause erupted as Dr. Kelly stepped up and shook hands with Mr. Campbell, then stood beside the lectern and began with an energetic greeting.

"Good evening, friends old and new. What a wonderful privilege you are giving me. This privilege began five years ago when I was driving through your community and saw cars parked everywhere, then saw from the bulletin board, why there were so many cars parked here on a Saturday morning. It was your Fall Kindness Breakfast Bazaar. So, I stopped and came in for breakfast. The breakfast was as good as any country breakfast I have ever eaten anywhere, but what surpassed that was the friendship and atmosphere which energized this place and still signals the reason you keep having your kindness bazaars. It's all an expression of what your minister calls simply, friendship ministry, and is a very unique way you build the funds you use to extend your friendship and kindness ministry. What you are putting into practice in real time, is a working expression of my ideas about what is central in our best and most inclusive identity base, oneness, and what I call, the new sacred. I welcome the opportunity to have a part in the varied ministries you have going here.

Reverend Carvelle told me about your program ministry, as he showed me around your excellent newly expanded conference facilities where you carry out your multiple programs. He talked about Dr. Ray Hart, who, when he retired from teaching and being program director for a large church, came here and began to build a vision which has grown into the finest expression of program ministry I have ever seen in any church, large or small. I am honored to come and be a part of it. I think your church may be at the growing edge of an important new model for any church in our time, in which the identity and mission are becoming less theological and more humanitarian.

Perhaps it would be good if I told you about my first connection with your church and my first meeting with Dewey Campbell. Let me tell you about it as an inexact verbatim that's easy to remember, and as though you had never even heard about this place - just like you were standing off and looking in on that special morning.

I was driving through the country one beautiful fall morning, when I came upon a site that made me wonder, *what is going on here?* On the slope of the hill stood a white weatherboard church with a modest steeple on the top front center. The central sanctuary was flanked by a wing to one side, accessed by a glassed-in connecting breezeway, which appeared to be a fellowship hall and classrooms. I could see people going in and coming out there.

Cars were parked all over the place, I mean all over the place, way out beyond the parking lot, all the way out beyond the cemetery, and down to the road. Sometimes funerals draw big crowds like that, but this was eight o'clock on Saturday morning. I thought, there might be a big banner to tell what was going on, but there wasn't. I slowed down enough to be sure I could read the bulletin board. The name, Center Church, was on the top, and in the center, it simply said, KINDNESS BREAKFAST BAZAAR.

In my mind, I said, *"there's gotta be a story here."* so I stopped. I had already eaten my bowl of cereal for breakfast, but I reasoned that I could eat again. I finally found a parking spot down on the road and got out. As I walked up toward the church, I met several people coming out. I stopped one man, and said, 'Good morning. Quite a gathering. May I ask what's happening?'

'Oh, it's the semi-annual Kindness Breakfast Bazaar,' the man replied. 'This one is the Fall Bazaar, with an emphasis on Christmas. They have one in the spring, called the Festival of Spring. It focuses on all the wonders of nature. It's an event like no other in this community.'

I queried further, 'You said, "they." Aren't you a member of this church?'

'Oh, no,' came the quiet and thoughtful answer, 'But I wouldn't mind being a part of a church with this kind of mission.'

'Mission? This is a mission?' I quizzed, for further explanation. 'What is the driving force?'

'You going in for breakfast?' he asked as a return question.

'Yes,' I answered summarily.

'Well, you can get a better answer if you will find Dewey Campbell. Get him to sit down with you. He'll tell you the story with enthusiasm, like he was telling it for the very first time, and like you had never heard it. You must not be from around here,' the man said, more as an inquiry than statement.

'I am not too far away. But, I would like to know more. Thanks for your help,' I said, as I started toward the big wing unit on the side of the church.

There was a line of people going by an elaborate country breakfast buffet. I got in line and began looking around. A perimeter of tables surrounded the area where people were eating. The surrounding tables were filled with bazaar items with a Christmas theme. People were making their selections. I spoke to the people in front of me and said, 'I was told that I could find out more about this event if I would find Dewey Campbell. Is he here?' I asked.

'Right over there,' came the simple reply, as the man pointed.

As soon as I got my plate filled with country breakfast foods, I headed over to the table. 'May I join you?' I asked, without setting my plate down.

'Be glad to have you,' he said, and picked up his coffee cup to take a sip. 'This your first time here?' he asked, with a gentle smile on his sun-tanned face.

'Yes. I saw all these cars and decided to stop in. And I was told I could ask you about this event.'

'Well,' he said, pushing his plate to one side and putting his coffee cup in front of him, 'It goes back a ways. See, we are a small church and usually we get young preachers, or preachers ready to retire. One year, they sent us a preacher just out of seminary. He was single and all the young ladies took a liking to him. But that's not the main thing that got our attention. He had this idea that kindness ought to be the defining quality of our faith. He preached a sermon about it soon after he got here. He said, 'There are some personal qualities which should overarch everything else about our faith.' I remember a few of those qualities, caring, honesty, and nobility, with the leading quality being kindness. I was sitting beside of Carl Akin and his wife, Judy, that Sunday. Carl is a successful young businessman. Judy is a Life Sciences teacher. Soon as church was over, I said, 'Carl and Judy, I wonder if there is some way we could put legs to that sermon. I mean, find a way to make what the preacher said, the centerpiece of who we are in this church.' I said, 'I'm not saying that we don't already have a lot of what he talked about, but how could we take it a step beyond that? And I have an idea. How about if we ask the preacher to go to lunch with us at Long's Restaurant and explore some ideas?'

Well, we did just that, and the preacher was more than open to the question when I asked, 'Preacher, how could we put legs to your sermon? I mean, how can we make the kindness you talked about a real part of what we do here?'

Now I don't need to explain much more than ask you to look at what's happening here this morning. Well, I can explain a little more.' Pointing, he said, 'There are Carl and Judy, right over there. And right over there is the preacher. Wonder why he has all those young ladies at his table. You ought to ask him about that sermon, and several others. But, he used a couple of big words to help us focus on what he said that Jesus was all about. He said, 'transcendence, is about God up in the spiritual realm, and is what most people's religion is about - praising God and trying to be in good standing with him.' But, he said, 'Jesus was focused on the other side of that - on immanence - on what we need to be doing down here in everyday life.' He said, 'people talked about Jesus as a man who "went about doing good," and that should be what we are all about.'

'Am I telling you too much?' Mr. Campbell asked, as he paused and took a sip of coffee.

'Not at all,' I said. 'Keep going.'

So, Carl, Judy, and the preacher, and I sat there at the restaurant and tried to figure out two things – how we could multiply kindness right here in this community, and how we could come up with a plan to finance our ideas. It was the preacher who said, that every member of this church should see himself or herself as an ambassador of kindness, right here in the church, in their home, in this community, in their work – reaching out with kindness in a thousand different ways. We should preach it, teach it, and live it as though that's who we are – who we really are.' The preacher can explain this better than I, so go over and talk to him after a while. When you talk to him, I know one thing he'll say, which he repeats often. He'll say, 'the church has been long on transcendence, and short on immanence, and we need to reverse that.'

But it was Carl and Judy who really put the legs to his ideas. And this bazaar is a result. It was their idea. So, we raise money here that we use only to express some kind of kindness and compassion right here where we all live and work. If we find somebody who needs help, we are organized to be there, and to find out how we can help. See these young people serving the tables, they are this idea in real time. They are trained for what they do as their mission of kindness. Judy trains them. She's a Life Sciences teacher and trains them how to serve properly. But more than that, she tells them to put kindness at the center. They are to speak with kindness, and act with kindness in everything they do, as they serve.'

One of the youth servers came over and said, "Mr. Campbell, may I refresh your coffee?"

"Oh, thank you, Charlene," he said cordially, extending his cup, then kept right on talking with enthusiasm. He said, 'You ought to see this place when we have our Spring Bazaar. All kinds of plants and garden ideas everywhere. We have two or three sessions before the bazaar – someone who knows the science of agriculture comes out to talk. And we have other sessions which focus on science, especially environmental science. All during the year we have classes and seminars on health, psychology, economics, gardening, even farming. We draw on local talent, and bring in people who have special knowledge about various fields. And when we bring in outstanding speakers, this place is crowded. Cars parked all over the place. Like today. All the speakers we bring in help us to make better decisions about life.'"

Dr. Kelly paused a moment in his recall of Mr. Campbell's enthusiastic story. He explained, "I have had to do verbatim at times when it was hard to remember what was said, but in this case it was easy. Mr. Campbell was so caught up in telling about the program of his church that I just sat there listening, enthralled.

Mr Campbell continued." 'It's all part of the preacher's main idea. Our preacher says, that our faith ought to be one with our science and technology; they both should recognize the sacred nature of all existence. We should be informed and guided by our best human qualities so that, in our unparalleled time in history, we are reaching for a higher humanity.' You couldn't help but be inspired if you heard his sermons.'

Mr. Campbell slowed down a bit, but kept going. He said, 'You would be impressed with some of the high level science oriented teachers and speakers we have all through the year, who come here to help us understand the way our faith needs to be updated so it has integrity with our growing knowledge base - so we become, not just techno-humans, but better humans.

But, dropping back a bit to that Sunday, following our very first Kindness Bazaar, the atmosphere here was charged with a new energy. You could feel it. I don't remember our young preacher's sermon that Sunday, but I do remember his benediction. He simply said, 'What a great time we have had together. Keep it going.' That's what he said - 'Keep it going.' We had a new identity. We had a new mission - kindness. Kindness in all we do!

So, what you see here is an idea being lived out. And it keeps expanding in terms of how we can instill kindness in all we do. This has energized this church in ways far beyond our bazaars. The church has a respect in this community which makes people want to be a part of this idea, and, in fact, to become a member of this church. The church has grown in membership. But more important than that, we have grown in our understanding, not so much about who God is, but in who we are, so that kindness and caring are at the center of our faith.

We don't even advertise this event. It speaks for itself. Everybody in this community know about it. They want to be a part of it. People who aren't even members of this church, make things for the bazaar, and then come and buy things others have made, then give them away. It's rather contagious. See, we have one rule. Not one penny of the money raised can be used for the church. It all has to be expressed in some act of kindness to others around us. So we are always looking for ways we can help. And, it is just understood, that what we do as acts of kindness is always to be done quietly. Of course, good chance of that; you can't keep things like that a secret. The stories just leak out.

And that's it. That's what you see here. Well, there's a lot more to it, but that's what we keep trying to do - to make kindness the centerpiece of who we are and what we are about.'

Just then a man came up and sat down beside Mr. Campbell and interrupted. But Mr. Campbell turned back to me and said, 'Why don't you go over and talk to the preacher. You'll have to cut in. Those young ladies keep him occupied. And why don't you find Carl and Judy and talk to them.

But before you go, let me show you something Drew had in the bulletin this past Sunday. You can have it, but let me read a paragraph.'

Mr. Campbell pulled the tightly folded and crumpled copy out of his shirt pocket and began reading.

Too many people discredit themselves in our times, not because they are under the umbrella of being Jewish, Christian, Moslem, or some other religion, but because they have no overarching sunrise vision that lights the way to see and respect the oneness of all existence and their place in that story. The great need of our time is for world citizens, who live out humanity's highest qualities in their own time and place, no matter what their religion.

Mr. Campbell handed it to me and said, 'Pretty good isn't it? Take it with you. Maybe you can use it some way.'

I did talk to Reverend Carvelle, and learned more from Carl and Judy. As I look out across the audience, I see Carl and Judy here tonight and I congratulate them, as I congratulate all of you on your ongoing story. And, in turn, my own story will never be the same. I have been here for each of your Kindness Breakfast Bazaars since then. And now, here I am, like I just stepped into that story again, and am so pleased that I can be here. But right now, what I must do is begin talking about what I was asked to talk about for the next four evenings - my writing.

As I begin, I want to say up front that there is one important inclusive word that I use often. Identity. Who are we? Who can we be? And, also, who should we be, lest we shortchange ourselves and the earth family. It has to do with trying to be great citizens. We have great cities across the world, great agriculture, great transportation, and great communication. But more and more, especially in our rapidly changing age, we need to define who we are by qualities that develop the best persons we can be, lest we betray our potential, lest we fail to build talents and relationships that reward us with energizing, wholesome returns. Our identity needs to have a positive, rewarding, working return. We also need to know who we are in our digital-molecular-information age so we link our identity with the growing knowledge base that helps us align with the oneness of all molecular existence.

My working thesis has to do with identity. A major paradigm shift is occurring in our time in history. We are crossing a great divide from an authority-based religion, informed by mythology, sacred texts, and tradition, over to a knowledge-based faith, in-formed by science and technology and by the highest qualities of our humanity. It's not just what evolution and the march of civilization have made us, although we certainly wouldn't be here in this grand age of technology without that, but what we now make of ourselves, that is what is so critical at this juncture of the human story. The endowment of the ages and the progression of knowledge have placed new expectations on our shoulders as an obligation of high privilege. It's in that paradigm phrase, *noblesse oblige*. Nobility obligates. If we are to free ourselves from the grip of the past, new generations must be ready to hear a call from the future, then take a responsible place in it. That growing identity is sacred.

What we believe, how we think, the choices we make, and the way we live, should reflect the uniqueness of our humanity, especially in our time and place in the story of civilization. New advances in knowledge of the molecular nature of all existence, macro or micro, should be integrated into our faith as an open-ended way to respect the God of all molecular existence. That's a call from the future to which we can respond. It is an ongoing echo of the vision of Isaiah, who asked, "Whom shall I send, and who will go for us?" Then I said, "Here I am. Send me." (Isaiah 6:8 RSV) So we hear the call - a call to fulfill the highest humanity we know, right in our own story we are writing. It's a call to each individual. Nobody else can make the response for us. It's up to us. It's a critical call to today's new generation. It's a call to the earth family. It's the call to which millions can respond and say, "Here am I. Send me."

As I share the ideas I am putting together in my writings, I want you to feel that we are doing interactive thinking and exploring together - that we are a little think tank. So, I want you to participate by asking questions and sharing ideas at any time. Just put up your hand, or just jump in and say, "But, Dr. Kelly, what about....." I want to make this an interdisciplinary dialogue, crossing over the many careers and activities in which you are engaged, and the insights that grow out of the roles you play in your work, homes, and community. Yes, I will probably do most of the talking. But just knowing that we can be interactive draws out what I have to say. But I still want you to be a part of it, so that we are all engaged in the best thinking we can do. I think you should know that I welcome questions following a session, also. I am always glad to stay around and talk as long as you want to talk. So, don't hesitate. I am never in a hurry to leave this place. It's in these "standing-around-times" that we often have our best exchange of ideas.

Let me ask the first question. "Where are we?" No, it's not like what they said of Columbus, that when he set out, he didn't know where he was going, and when he got there he didn't know where he was, and when he got back home, he didn't know where he had been. Informed by the progression of knowledge and explorations in astronomy, we are learning more about where we are. We are on a little planet that sits way out on an outer arm of the Milky Way Galaxy, which is but one of billions of galaxies in the universe that is so expansive we don't know yet where it all stops, if it does. So, that's where we are. Somewhere in infinity.

But where are we in terms of planet earth, and the time frame in which we live, and in humanity's lengthening story and growing knowledge base? In the long view of the successive ages of human civilization, we have just arrived in the digital-molecular-information age. We are exploring and designing at the smallest entities of existence - atoms and their components, on down to quartz, and beyond. This makes it a new renaissance, the age of new levels of understanding and communication, the age of the internet and the ubiquitous cell phone. We have left the stone age, and 'the world is flat' age, and moved into the age of nano-science and nano-technology. And hopefully we have crossed over into the knowledge age, and the age of new accountability, characterized increasingly by our moving into the age of sustainable development - the green age, if you please. I say, hopefully, because the support base for this needs to be progressive and transition to sources of energy like wind and solar and other sources yet to be discovered and developed. I don't share the apocalyptic view that 'the sky is falling,' but

I do believe we are becoming aware of the need for new paradigms of what constitutes a sustainable future and the wisest future we can dream and design. We may have dug a hole for ourselves, but I am told that, when we discover that the hole we are digging is already too deep, what we are supposed to do is, stop digging. And, one of my hopes for the church of our time is that its leaders will help us to know how to stop digging, and find out how to define human identity on the knowledge-based side of a great divide that can be extended far into a wise and sustainable tomorrow. It is a major opportunity for the church to help us address some of the great causes of humanity - to find new paradigms which launch us into better tomorrows than our yesterdays. That, I believe, is a commanding mission for the church of our time. It's call from the future. It's the new sacred.

But what we have right now is a time for a break and refreshments. I understand that volunteers have refreshments that are ready. So, let's break for a few minutes. When you hear Cassie Lou Hall playing the piano, that's a signal to gather back to continue our session."

CHAPTER TWO

Sunrise Horizons!

If there is a new sacred, there must be an old sacred.
What's the difference? And why does it matter?"

As soon as the people had gathered back to their seats, Dr. Kelly said, "What I know is that somebody here knows how to bake cookies, down-home style. Thanks to all who provided our refreshments. Now, with our new surge of energy, let's talk about transcendence and immanence, and about the new sacred.

First and foremost, I am a teacher. I not only continue teaching at the university, but I teach a Sunday School class of young adults, so you can be sure I am familiar with people asking questions. And I always welcome them. And I welcome yours. We face some big, tough questions in our time and they deserve a bold, open, honest response that goes beyond pat answers. A teacher who has integrity with the progression of the human story must respect the past, but respect the future even more. Teaching requires honesty with facts, but also honesty with vision. I have a model for my teaching. It is set by the Master Teacher of Galilee, whose teaching required both honesty and courage to announce a better future.

My vision for the future of the human story is focused in ten words that form an important template for the new sacred. I will come to those defining words soon, as a recurring theme in all I have to say, but right now I want to open the floor to questions."

Immediately a young lady stood and said, 'Dr. Kelly, you talk about the new sacred. If there is a new sacred, there must be an old sacred. What's the difference? And why does it matter?'

Dr. Kelly walked nearer and said, "I am sure the people here know your name, but I would like to know it, so I am not just be answering the question, but talking to a person, who couldn't have asked a better question to begin this session."

'My name is Beverly, but most people just call me Bev, and that's fine with me.'

Dr. Kelly paused with a broad smile and said, "Bev, that's such a great question that I wish you would please tell your friends that I didn't set you up to ask this question."

'There was no set up,' Bev said. 'Just a real interest. I am a teacher, also, and I like that term, the new sacred. I want to know more about it, especially the difference.'

"The difference? The contrast? It's how you look at things. But more importantly, how we look at things has taken such a quantum leap, in our age of science and technology, that it calls for us to make a major step forward in our identity.

Sometimes metaphors get stretched so far that they add to more confusion than clarify. But I like to refer to the metaphorical story of Moses as he stood with his throngs of people at the edge of the Red Sea, wondering what to do, now that the Egyptian army was pursuing them from behind and the Red Sea was blocking the way in front of them. It was like Moses had led them to a dead end. Betrayed. Nobody had even been asked to bring a single boat. In panic, they were thinking that they would have been better off if they had never followed their dreams. Surely the dreamer, Moses, was a fool! But was he? He knew this territory. He had been here before when he had escaped from Egypt and fled to the land of Midian.

One interpretation of the story is that Moses held up his staff and the Red Sea began to roll back on two sides, like walls of water, to make a path through the sea. You know, like Cecil B. De Mille depicted in the movie, "The Ten Commandments." They needed a God to rescue them, or else this was the end of the story – the end of their great dreams about being free.

But there were options, and Moses knew about them. It was time to rely upon knowledge. In that interpretation Moses had looked ahead and had already put his knowledge of the Red Sea and his dreams together. One little statement in the story tells about how a strong east wind blew all night long. By the next morning the tide had moved far out leaving that area as a sandy peninsula. In the sunrise of a new day, Moses lifted his staff and said, "Let's march!"

The story became a major metaphor for what people can do when they are up against new unknowns and need to work with the way the world works out of the progression of knowledge and out of a sunrise vision of great dreams. Part of the new sacred, therefore, is to learn all we can about the way the world works and learn to work with the way it works. The new sacred has to do with using the platform of knowledge we are able to access through our new tools in our time. But what makes that important is how we can direct and use our knowledge and our new tools so we are better people and live a better life! That is the new sacred that is up to us.

So, we stand at the edge of the Red Sea. It's time for us to put our knowledge-based faith together with what we are learning about the way the world works, and do what we can to build our greatest dreams for a great future and noble humanity, and give them their best chance to come true. That's the new sacred!

The difference? It doesn't change the past, but it does change and reshape the future. It opens up a whole new story that we can write. It lets us use the gifts of the mind, combined with great dreams, to define who we are and what we can do to turn old endings into new beginnings. That's the difference. It's the story we can write that is expected of us in this fantastic age of opportunity where nobility obligates, where we can build the greatest new tomorrows the world family has ever known. We can learn forward. We learn as we go and go as we learn. It's a difference that is up to us!

While I am turning old stories into metaphors, let me tell you about that Hebrew nation many years later, after they had become a young nation, but not yet big enough and strong enough that they could hold off an attack from the Babylonian army. As a result, they were overrun and many of the Hebrew people were taken off to Babylon where they were to be slaves. With a different challenge in a different time, they were at the Red Sea again. So much for, 'the promised land' of 'milk and honey.' They felt betrayed by their dreams. They were captives in a foreign land. So, what did they do? They looked back on yesterday and cherished the good old days. A psalmist wrote about their plight and their lack of vision and hope.

> By the waters of Babylon
>   there we sat down and wept,
>   when we remembered Zion.
> On the willows there
>   we hung our lyres,
> For there our captors
>   required of us songs,
> And our tormentors, mirth, saying,
>   'Sing us one of the songs of Zion!'
>   Psalms 137:1–3 RSV

Opportunity was just waiting! They could sing in a new land and make it into a new time and place to sing about the sunrise of faith - turn their problems into opportunity. The Babylonians had heard about their singing and wanted to hear them sing. But, no. They wouldn't sing. They were too caught up in yesterday to sing a new song today. Yesterday was the golden age. Today was the depression age. Defined by the past, they hung their harps on willow trees, waiting for a miracle - waiting for deliverance to come, just when they could have been building dreams and singing the songs of Zion in their un-chosen land.

It's an approach to life that reappears in our time - people refusing to see the good in today because they are locked in yesterday - never looking at life in terms of the wonders of what they have been gifted to do for themselves on the sunrise horizon of new dreams of new tomorrows - never singing about the wonders of life in this new arena of opportunity.

But Louis Armstrong dared to look at life and see new opportunity. He sang,

> I see skies of blue …. clouds of white
> Bright blessed days … dark sacred nights
> And I think to myself …. what a wonderful world.[1]

The difference? It's the way we think. It's the way we reset the brain and magnetize it to look for ways we can align science and technologies with the Big Ten Universal Qualities so they will guide us to write the greatest humanitarian story for the common good the human family has ever written. We can't change yesterday, but today is still open! If we want to live in a wonderful world, we must do what we can to make it a wonderful world. It's up to us. The paradigm is not transcendence. It's immanence. It's our time in history.

Why is it important? It's because the future we ask for becomes our request of life and defines our place in the story. We set our

---

[1]   Louis Armstrong Memory Lane Music Group

expectations by the vision we see – by what we dream – by what we plan to give to life!

It's the same world in which Jesus said, 'the kingdom of heaven is at hand.' He announced the promise of the future as one that people could, not only dream about, but make real now. So the Teacher from Nazareth defined opportunity, not by what we can't do, but by what we can do when we live forward. Instead of 'thou shalt not,' he said, 'Blessed are those who hunger and thirst for righteousness.' And 'Blessed are the peacemakers.' 'You are the salt of the earth.' 'You are the light of the world.' Lead the way. Turn a light on in the darkness. The guidance from the Teacher lives on. We hear his call anew in this new age. It's our time to play our harps and sing, 'It's a wonderful world.'

In that spirit, the pioneers came across the ocean to Ellis Island, looking for the new world. And they didn't stop there. It wasn't long before that pioneering spirit made them set out for the west on new frontiers. They lined up their wagons and said, "westward, ho!"

It's our time now. It's time for the people of a knowledge-based faith in the digital-information-molecular age to use their cell phones and text about new beginnings beyond old endings – time to give their best dreams their best chance to happen in our story. We are the ones to make the new sacred real. We are the Big Ten Generation.

The Big Ten Universal Qualities are words that can be chosen by anyone, anywhere, at anytime for the most wholesome, rewarding life one can live! The Big Ten can be taught in all the learning centers of the world. Children can grow up with this understanding of who they are called to be – people of nobility and excellence. This template of identity needs to be taught in our homes, schools, churches, video games, television programs, movies, in pulpits, in classrooms, and in the books we read – until we gain a new vision of being Big Ten world citizens. These ten words should be taught in many ways in an endless variety of settings, until no child is left behind, until there can be no child anywhere who has never heard of the Big Ten Universal Qualities. It's a grand age for dreaming, a grand time for venturing into the sunrise of new tomorrows.

In the old garden story, Eve faced the negative advice of the storyteller of old, telling her, 'Don't risk – don't test the edge of the possible – don't venture – just accept what you've been told – don't you dare taste those apples.' But in the spirit of all that was right about Eve, and exercising the freedom that she had been given to make choices, she reached up and picked up one of those apples. It was good! She gave one to Adam. The future was theirs to choose and they chose it. That's the new sacred.

Now let me slow down a little bit and get out of the oratorical style and explain in more detail.

The old sacred is based in transcendent authority. It is informed by ancient mythologies which were attempts to answer big questions in early times about how God makes the world work, but with only very limited knowledge about how the world really works. They didn't have science, just stories, handed down across the centuries to bring old answers forward to a different time, with very little update. And so the mythologies and traditions of the old sacred were put together in books, which are now considered so sacred they must never be questioned. In short, the old sacred was on the holding edge of the past, and all the more revered by some, because it was that – the holding edge.

In contrast, the new sacred is on the leading edge of the future. In the new sacred, we embrace and respect humanity's progression of knowledge, acutely aware of how rapidly that knowledge is advancing in what is now networked into big data and digital collective intelligence. That knowledge base has expanded so much that now science and new technologies are inseparable, and not one of us wants to live without these advantages.

When we go to a modern hospital, we expect that the skilled people there will utilize the latest knowledge in science and its computer-based tools. Nobody in our time wants to have surgery where the doctors are not aligned with the latest in medical science and its tools. So, the new sacred respects this advance in knowledge, joined with technology.

While we recognize the metaphorical value of sacred texts and do not want to be without these classic old stories, if we are honest, we will recognize the old sacred for what it was, and is, early stages of knowledge about God, about the world, about the universe, and about humanity.

For some, it is arrogant, even heresy, to go beyond the old sacred, with its rules and mandates from the past. But for others, it is a necessary expansion of faith to go beyond that in order to be honest and have respect for the progression of the gifts of the mind and hand. We are only in an early stage of this infusion of knowledge and its interface with the tools of technology, so it is very important that our faith be open-ended as a framework for our future identity.

There are ten defining qualities that form a framework for a future oriented faith. I call them the Big Ten. There are, of course, more than ten, but I name ten which are so basic that they can apply in all the varied cultures in our world family. And besides, even as smart as we are, ten is about all we can remember and measure by on a checks-and-balances basis. These qualities have no boundaries in politics, geography, religion, ethnic orientation, or social customs. They are universal qualities and embraceable by all people, anytime, anywhere in all the world family, especially in our age of globalization. These universal qualities are not a new authority to replace the old. They are open-ended and overarching dimensions of a faith that can be chosen over and above other identity markers of politics, culture, and religion, or no religion These define us at the growing edge of our information age, where new knowledge continues to add both new revelation and practical guidance.

With the increase of new revelations, we are more and more aware that there is a God that links the mystery of whatever causes and sustains all molecular existence, the "Eveready Battery", that keeps on going and going, mysteriously re-energizing itself without a microsecond of fatigue or delay for millions of years! Respect for that, in whatever ways we can learn about it and describe it in our time in the story, is the new sacred!

As for the old sacred, you know about it already. Some of you have heard it all your life. You are told that it's taught in the Bible and tradition, and you just must never change it, or even question it. It's sacred just like it is, even though it is taught in one way by one church on the street, and in another way by a different church on down the same street. As different as each of these may be, you have been told that if you don't believe what is taught, you may be in serious trouble with God.

So, in that old sacred paradigm, there is a transcendent God somewhere in heaven. And if you don't keep the commands of God, or obey his will, you need to bow in humble subservience, confess your sins, and beg God for his forgiveness, and that soon. You are assured that you can get that forgiveness because Jesus became the sacrifice for your sins, and if you appeal for forgiveness in his name, your sins will be washed away, and you'll be okay again. But be careful. You can get in trouble again and need to get forgiveness again before sundown. What is silently happening, in this sweeping paradigm, is that you are looking backwards on life and always trying to straighten out the past, instead of looking forward and building the future as a magnetic forward-reaching set of dreams and expectations.

In so many churches, the old sacred is echoed and reinforced in the hymns they sing, describing how God's penalizing anger goes on forever, unless it is absolved in some way. So they reinforce this old mythological heaven-to-earth paradigm by singing again and again, songs such as "How Great Thou Art."

> And when I think that God, his Son not sparing,
> sent him to die, I scarce can take it in;

that on the cross, my burden bearing,
he bled and died to take away my sin;[2]

To some people, this viewpoint is sacred, and if you don't believe it, that is one more sin that gets added to your list. Of course,
it doesn't take a lot of sins for you to be in trouble with God. One
will do. It is a transcendence view of God and results in human
beings seeing themselves as servile slaves, who only escape God's
wrath if they bow in submission, beg forgiveness, then praise him
again and again, and obey his every command as it has been shaped
by mythology and tradition, and then set forth in sacred texts.

When a person holds rigidly to that transcendence view of
religion, the big words are apology, confession, forgiveness, and
praise. It embodies surrendering to the will of an authority, where
if you break the rules, you have broken relationship with God and
he is angry, defensive, even vengeful, and you must do something
to get back into his favor. So, you come on hands and knees in
subservience.

In significant contrast, the new sacred is an immanence based
paradigm, where we are in a working partnership with the forces
of all cosmic existence and are always learning and seeking to
understand, cooperate, and find better ways to fulfill a working
partnership. The forces are impartial and no apology is needed, just
correction of what you discover doesn't work right. What is needed
is for us to discover the way the world works, then work with the
way the world works to the best of our ability as an important
part of a knowledge-based faith. It's a continuous learning process
in which we respect the working nature of all facets of molecular
existence, including ourselves, especially including ourselves. It's
where updating our faith means being open-ended, exploratory,
and future oriented.

---

[2]   Stuart K Hine

Our opportunity then, is to live on the growing edge of the future and the knowledge-based side of a credible faith for our time in history. Instead of an identity of escape and singing about heaven, "when we've been there ten thousand years," we can live so that we make the best of life, here for "ten thousand years," or for one year, or one day. So we sing,

> This is a day of new beginning,
> time to remember and move on,
> time to believe what love is bringing,
> laying to rest the pain that's gone.[3]

A SUNRISE VISION FAITH!

At this point of civilization's progressive story, the church cannot be forgiven if it clings to the old sacred systematic theology, instead of moving on to sunrise vision, in which the future expectations we set for ourselves become our request of life. A church that serves the best interests of its people will embrace the call of the future, and respect it as, vision from tomorrow. In the new sacred, ministers will be prophets of honor when they are spokespersons on behalf of the greatest causes of a higher humanity and a greater tomorrow. Church members will fulfill their call from the future when they make the Big Ten qualities their template for identity in all of their daily living. It's a call from the future. It's the new sacred.

AN OVERARCHING FAITH

It is believed that there are more than one thousand religions in the world and many have some version of the old sacred, where the understanding is that one must appease God to be in his good favor by doing some kind of subservient living. Across the thousands of years, people have prayed endless prayers, tortured their bodies,

---

[3]   Brian Wren

gone without food, sacrificed their infant babies, washed in rivers, gone on pilgrimages, offered a continuing flow of gifts, and lifted their words in praise so they can be free from this sense that God is angry with them. They have assumed that God is like a king and they are his subjects who must obey and court his pleasure and favor. It becomes a prison for the mind.

There is a better way. We have crossed a great divide and know, as never before, that the God of all existence is not just a God of yesterday, but a God of open understandings and endless tomorrows.

I live with hope for the church that it's greatest days are ahead. I keep hoping we will stop postponing the great future to some far away fantasy place, most often called heaven, and do our best to make as much heaven as we can here. Even if it is a gradual and silent paradigm shift, that call from tomorrow is more to be desired than an oppressive captivity to yesterday.

The only time any of us ever have to achieve this is in this tiny window of time that we have in the earth story. Everything is always in a continuous state of molecular activity and change. We are a part of it. We have no guarantee that anything, or anyone, will escape the events that may occur in our universe, our galaxy, our solar system, or on the "pale blue dot" where we live. If this little planet gets too close to the sun, it will become too hot for human continuation. And if it gets too far away from our sun it will become a frozen planet. Or if an asteroid collides with the earth, some areas will become a barren wasteland. Our story is one with all the ongoing changes in the cosmos, one with a hundred billion galaxies, one with all the units of existence, including our little planet home. So far, we have little control over the larger events in our own solar system, much less in galaxies, where it takes a million light years to travel between its stars. So far, we are "sitting ducks" for collision from multiple space rocks, like the 2009 DD45, which came within forty-eight thousand miles of earth on March

2, 2009, and which, if it had hit the earth, would have impacted the earth similar to the meteorite which landed in Siberia in 1906. That collision devastated eight hundred square miles of forest. Even though we are now tracking space debris, we remain vulnerable because we are just a part of what's happening in space, near and far. What we do have, is a grand opportunity to play out the greatest qualities of humanity on the stage that we have been privileged to walk onto in our brief moment of time, in our tiny enclave in space. What we have is the greatest opportunity ever to shape the future by the progression of information and knowledge and quest for qualities-based living. The mission then, for the religions of the world, is to make the story we can now write in our molecular age into the greatest story ever written. That is the new sacred!

There are more of us now in the human family, and we are living longer than in any previous time in our human story. But making more of us who live longer does not necessarily equate with being wiser and better. Coming alive here, to a wiser human-ity and a more rewarding future, is our immediate opportunity and responsibility. It's the future we can ask for. It's the new sacred."

Dr. Kelly paused long enough that it seemed like a stopping place. Instead he said, "I have taken so long to respond to your question that others may be hesitant to ask further questions. But go ahead. Maybe I'll do better now."

In response, one man in his mid fifties stood up and said cau-tiously, "Dr. Kelly, I don't think you need to do better. That was good, but I have a question. It's one a lot of people are asking in our time of change. What I want to know is what do you believe, point-blank, is there a God, or not?"

Dr. Kelly answered slowly and without hesitation. "Point-blank, sir. And, your name is?"

"I am Harvey McGregor."

"Straight forward, Mr. McGregor, Yes. Yes, there is a God. There is a God of the mystery of all molecular existence. We may not be able to explain it, or to define that God. But yes, I believe in a mysterious God.

But, of course, not everybody understands God the same way, now, or ever have. What everyone calls, God, is different for every time in history, and in the mind of every person who tries to answer the question. And, it keeps changing, especially when we move beyond authority-based religion to an open-ended knowledge-based faith - from a sunset paradigm to sunrise paradigm. New insights are being added as we learn more about the working dynamics of all molecular existence. We are at a time in human thinking when we may need to reformulate our understandings of God. In our progression of paradigms, God is not only the God of a Big Bang yesterday, but of endless tomorrows and the progression of stories in between. Our concepts keep changing as we push back the edge of the possible. There is a God of marvel and wonder, of greater magnitude than we have words to imagine, define, or even find metaphors to suggest.

So, yes, there is a God, but our metaphors are so very limited. We no longer think of the gods as riding through the air up to Mount Olympus to talk with Zeus, the king of the gods, as in Greek mythology. Nor do we make God like us, as in early Hebrew thinking, like a warrior, a king, a judge, or shepherd, and even an angel-like person who is also a man, as in Christian tradition. We need more and better metaphors to help us think and talk about God now that we are beginning to understand something about the oneness of all molecular existence, and as we explore elementary particles on a new scale with the Large Hadron Collidor. Religious words must now cross over with words about micro scientific forces, and with words about macro galactic forces in endless space to give us even a hint of how to think and talk about God in ways which are honest, open, and respectful of the miracle of existence and our growing knowledge about the oneness of all existence.

Yes, there is a God that we are seeking to understand in new ways. Perhaps we do best when we think, not of a God who is above and beyond, but down here, within and linked with the mystery of existence, indefinable, even with our new and growing respect for the molecular nature of existence. It's in this arena that the human mind seeks to understand existence by using its own gifts, expanded now with computers and digital instruments of inquiry, to help us explore the micro and macro interrelated working forces that we are learning about in our time. It's a time when we are trying to understand more about our own molecular biology and the marvels of the brain. Our answer now must take account of Watson, Crick, Franklin and Wilkins for their discoveries of the DNA molecule. We must give considerable attention to the construction of the first self-replicating synthetic bacterial cell by the J Craig Venter Institute. In our neuroscience, we are exploring the ways the brain can be programmed to guide our choices so we become people of reverence and respect for the marvel and wonder of who we are and the story we can live out in our place on our little planet in the expanse of the cosmos.

The God that we are beginning to reference is beyond definition, but whose identity must include, why the combination of hydrogen and oxygen (H_2O) has kept water a part of the earth's phenomena for billions of years, why photosynthesis keeps working, why gravity has never forgotten a grain of sand, or the earth, or sun, or stars, or black energy for a nanosecond, and why a cohesion of elementary particles keeps planets and stars magnetically converged as units of existence billions of earth years – a God more fantastic than even science fiction can imagine or foreshadow in its stories of intergalactic visits into, or from, deep space, a God whose mystery of forces underlie our humanity and the human mind. It's in the scope of all this that we are trying to find our best metaphors which respect the open-ended nature and oneness of the mystery of existence.

I am reminded of what the eminent scientist, Carl Sagan said,

"A religion, old or new, that stressed the magnificence of the Universe as revealed by modern science might be able to draw forth reserves of reverence and awe hardly tapped by the conventional faiths."[4]

In our human attempt to understand God, in the long reaches of our human story, we have been transitioning successively from Zeus, as the king of the gods, to the God of Abraham, Isaac, and Jacob, to the God of Jesus, and Mohammed, to the God of Galileo, Lincoln, Neil Armstrong, and Buzz Aldrin and the first footprints on the moon, to a God we are seeking to respect in the progression of knowledge that may give us new hints about a God who sustains existence, so that H2O still continues to be water.

There is a God more mysterious and profound than we know how to talk about. Having crossed the great divide from a transcendence God, beyond existence, to a God of immanence, down here in the real world of molecular existence, it now seems that, bowing down to God in subservience, as in old sunset paradigms, is not as respectful as thinking of being in a sunrise partnership with the creative and expansive forces in all existence that we are now learning about.

As best we can understand God, we need not live in fear of God, but in a trusting alliance with all the working forces of existence we are learning about, and sometimes still call God. So, it is not wise for us to think we need to plead and beg forgiveness for our sins, as though God is offended and revengefully angry. Our sins are not against God, they are against ourselves. Our sins erode our sense of self-respect. They make us afraid to reach boldly for the upper levels of our potential. Our sins make us so afraid and untrusting that we cling to yesterday more than reach for our best tomorrow. We have never had a better time in history to reach for sunrise tomorrows where what we plan to give to life can reset the future we ask for by dreaming our best dreams.

---

[4]   Carl Sagan. *Pale Blue Dot. P 52*

We are not the best we can be. Not yet. We can write a better story than we have written so far.

> We rise by things that are 'neath our feet;
> By what we have mastered of good and gain;
> By the pride deposed and the passion slain,
> And the vanquished ills we hourly meet. [5]

---

[5]   "Gradatim" Josiah Gilbert Holland

CHAPTER THREE

Drawing A Big Circle

He drew a circle that shut me out -
Heretic, rebel, a thing to flout.
But love and I had the wit to win:
We drew a circle that took him in.

--- Edwin Markham

DR. KELLY OPENED THE SESSION SLIGHTLY APOLOGETIC, BUT TEAS-
ingly, by saying,, "I have done so much talking so far that I wonder
if there is anyone who will risk asking another question."

"Dr. Kelly," a young man interjected quickly to take advantage
of the offer to ask a question, "I am a college student and obviously
do lots of reading. I wish I could say I have read your books, but
I haven't. Not yet. But from what I am hearing, I realize that I
think like you think. But here's my situation. I have a roommate
who is so locked in by what you call the old sacred and systematic
theology, that I accuse him of being a member of the "flat world
society." In turn, he accuses me of being a new "Benedict Arnold"
traitor to the 'faith of our fathers' because I hold views similar to
yours. So, mostly we just tolerate each other. How can I talk to

him? Or, maybe I should say, how can I listen? Can you give me some advice?"

Dr. Kelly responded slowly and quietly, "I like your question. It's on target. It's so on target that I don't want to begin responding without asking you name."

"My name is Brett. Brett Butler. Sometimes people call me Rhett Butler. And I don't dislike it. Gives a bit of prestige to it."

"And, Brett, I kind of like the connection. You have some of Rhett Butler's grit and class in your question. And I have lots of sympathy for your situation. I, myself, have difficulty talking, or listening, to people who already know they are right and I am wrong, before I say anything. I am still trying to learn how to be big enough not to pre-judge another's ideas. Even if I think I may have better ideas and more in sync with honest and informed thinking, I try not to be elitist. It's not an easy achievement, and I have my limitations. Especially, I try not to depersonalize or de-monize the other person. More and more I realize I don't have the answers to our deepest questions. It's so very easy to fall into the trap of letting some other person put me on the defensive and to defend my ideas, instead of being a good listener, and just sharing with others as fellow explorers of life's probing, and yet unan-swered, questions. There is so much more that we need to learn, and can learn at our strategic time in the human story.

The bigger goal is to be an artist in communication, where you demonstrate the art of listening. And that's not easy. Don't argue. Don't rebut. Don't defend. Just propel an idea to the next level of exploration. Sometimes you can shift beyond confrontation and debate, over to an exchange of ideas, by simply asking a question that explores an idea from a different angle, or in a new direction, as a sincere listener and learner. You can say, 'Let me ask you a question. What do you think about...?' Or, if the discussion is between different religions, the discussion might be moved be-yond religion by saying, 'Beyond our respective religious ideas, what do you consider to be the greatest causes of our time?' Most people will be flattered to be asked a question like that. Not many people have that art of dialogue to be able to make that kind of switch, but you can be one of those rare persons who does, or who is reaching for it. It's collaboration on a one-to-one level, with the opportunity to lift the art of communication to that higher level right there in your dorm room, with your roommate as an audience of one.

It's a matter of identity. What do you want people to remember about you - that you are someone who argued them down, with the result that they like you less, perhaps even building in a silent resentment toward you? What's that old phrase, 'convince person against his will, and he's of the same opinion still?' Or, had you rather be known as someone who is kind and conciliatory enough to explore life's big ideas, instead of just an unbending defender of entrenched ideas? Do you want to be remembered as someone who respects others? Will it really matter who wins the little debates we can get into so quickly? What's another oft repeated phrase, 'It doesn't matter who wins or loses, it's how we play the game?' The assumption in that phrase is that we are playing a bigger game than the one where the score is always changing on the gymnasium scoreboard, it's the score we earn by how well we show how big and fair we are, how we did our best when we could have become angry and resentful and fowled out in defensive plays, just when offensive plays were needed. That's how we can win, even when we lose.

I know I have responded to your question with more answer than you thought the question needed. It's like the little boy who went to his mother and said, "Where did I come from?"

She thought, "*Oh, no. This is the big question.*" So she said, "Why don't you go ask your dad?"

So he went to his dad and said, "Dad, where did I come from?" His dad put down the paper he was reading and said, "Son, why don't you sit down for a moment. This may take a while."

But the little boy protested, "I don't want to sit down. I just want to know where I came from. Did I come from North Carolina or Virginia?"

So, I may be giving you more answer than your question is about. What I have done, is to use your question to frame a positive approach to an identity we can live by that promotes the Big Ten Universal Qualities: kindness, caring, honesty, respect, collaboration, tolerance, fairness, integrity, diplomacy, and nobility. If we can make these our identity markers we will have won on a big scoreboard.

No one has to be one hundred percent right to be a good person and to render a great service. Any of us may be wrong about something, but still be a good person, and over time, be someone who makes a great contribution to our human story. We may have different opinions and still be engaged in great common causes which make us worthy of our time in history and place in the story. That's the bigger contest to be won beyond differences. A safe bet is to look for the good in others more than who's right or wrong. We can have the special inclusive quality Edwin Markham defined in his little quatrain.

> He drew a circle that shut me out –
> Heretic, rebel, a thing to flout.
> But love and I had the wit to win:
> We drew a circle that took him in.[6]

What is of great importance in our own journey story is to do our best to draw big circles! In a sense, all of life is a chance to draw Big Ten circles. If you can do that there is a good chance both you and your roommate will be winners.

Is it easy? Not at all. And sometimes you will not do as well as you wish you had when you look back on it. But you can never go back and change one word you said. or one attitude you expressed.

---

[6]   Edwin Markham "Outwitted."

You may talk to yourself with disappointment and say, 'I wish I had not said...' but it doesn't change a thing. So, all you can do is to learn forward – to learn from the past and try to make the future better. You may get a new roommate. Both of you will graduate and may never see each other again. But there will be other "roommates" who can be just as much of a challenge to your ability to draw big circles and make the qualities of the Big Ten, the identity markers you live by.

Two men met in the mall and began talking religion. They obviously didn't agree with each other. After a few moments, the debate became so intense that the man who was carrying his Bible, hit the other man over the head with his Bible. So, you'll meet your "roommate" again, and he may be so confrontational that it will take all the skill and diplomacy you can create to live up to your self-chosen identity markets of kindness, respect, and tolerance. You may meet the roommates who are certain that you are going straight to hell for what you believe, and have no reluctance in telling you that's where you are going. And you may feel like you have just been hit over the head with someone's Bible. That's when it becomes a test of your diplomacy and your ability to be kind and caring. It's your moment of test – your opportunity to show tolerance and fairness, and to draw a big enough circle to include that person in your winning circle. Again, is it easy? No. Not at all. And if, and when, you fail to pass the test, it's time to learn from your failure and still make the Big Ten Universal Qualities into your "checks and balances" guiding identity, and to keep learning forward to draw big circles.

I want to tell you about something from my childhood. In those days, they used to have community prayer meetings that met in the homes of people, or out on the porch, or in the yard on hot summer evenings. Nobody had air conditioning in those days. Nobody had to dress up. One could come in overalls and barefooted as children. It was very informal. My parents used to go to some of those meetings and drag us children along. It wasn't one of the things we bragged about to our friends the next day. At some point in the service, they might break out into a song that was so easy to sing anyone could join in. The song awakened several personifications as it progressed. They sang:

"Tis the old time religion, 'tis the old time religion, 'tis the old time religion, it's good enough for me.

It was good for Paul and Silas, it was good for Paul and Silas, it was good for Paul and Silas, and it's good enough for me.

It was good for our fathers, it was good for our fathers, it was good for our fathers, and it's good enough for me."

By this time, I felt like I had been hit over the head with religion and had better adopt this religion from the past. But then, the old song went on to refer to someone whose faith was more than a religion - a person who was loved and admired by everyone who knew her just as, Aunt Sarah, without knowing anything about her religion.

They sang, "It was good for old aunt Sarah, it was good for old aunt Sarah, it was good for old aunt Sarah, and it's good enough for me."

It would go on and on. The old song usually included a phrase like, "Makes the Methodist love the Baptist." or "Makes me love everybody, makes me love everybody, makes me love everybody, and it's good enough for me."

So, what they sang about was not actually "the old time religion" - just a living faith that got tested in the crucible of everyday life. Their 'religion' had changed before they got to it. They changed it for their times, even if they wouldn't admit it. Their children will change it yet again. Their theology was not something that any two of them would have agreed upon. But the faith they sang about, was a dynamic faith that helped them find strength in the trials and tribulations. They sang about a faith that gave them lift and courage in the face of life's struggles, and to which they could testify with joy and certainty as a celebration of the triumph of faith.

If they had been a part of the black tradition, their songs would have affirmed their courage and hope in the face of long and difficult struggle. It would have been in character with,

> "We shall overcome, we shall overcome, we shall overcome some day! Oh, deep in my heart I do believe we shall overcome some day!"

Or, they would have sung,

> "Sing a song full of the faith that the dark past has taught us; sing a song full of the hope that the present has brought us; facing the rising sun of our new day begun, let us march on till victory is won." [7]

At that prayer service, long years ago, we sat on the porch of a farmer who was among the successful farmers in that community, and with a house that was big enough that it announced his success. He didn't have one of those big John Deere tractors like farmers use now, but he had the latest farm tools for that time. Farming was still farming. And faith was still faith, no matter what religion it overarched.

We need an old time religion like that - a big circles faith - a faith that doesn't need a name - just a dynamic overarching template of identity where we put our knowledge and our faith together and draw big circles. And even if it is called "the old time religion," it doesn't matter all that much. What does matter is that we find our own working faith. That's the new sacred."

---

[7] James Weldon Johnson

CHAPTER FOUR

Measuring By Excellence

DEWEY CAMPBELL STEPPED TO THE LECTERN, ENERGIZED BY HIS privileged opportunity to announce the opening of the session in a special way. He began immediately, "I had the distinct privilege of presenting Dr. Kelly in the opening session of our conference. Now I have the distinct privilege of presenting two persons who will present our speaker for this session. You know them already, so I need only to ask these two young people to come forward and make their presentation. But still, I want to present them to you. They are Charlie West, and Julia Holtzcamp."

Mr. Campbell shook hands with them as they arrived, then stood beside them. He said, "How can I help but show my pride. These two young people are a part of the youth group here at the church. They let me be their counselor and tolerate my volleyball skills, or they might say, lack of skills. All these young people are my special friends. They have chosen Julia and Charlie to represent them in a presentation of our speaker. And, yes, they know Dr. Kelly. I saw them, along with other youth, standing around and talking with Dr. Kelly at the close of our last session, listening and asking questions with eagerness and respect. 'Julia, I understand you get to speak first.'"

Confidence and excitement were in her very first words as she said, "All of us in our group know we have a friend in our youth counselor, Mr. Campbell. And for him to ask us to present our speaker is an indication of how special that friendship is. He's the kind of person we would have in mind if we sang Carole King's song, "You've Got A Friend." We have a friend in Mr. Campbell. We have found another special friend in the person we welcome and present as our special speaker this evening. As Dr. Kelly talked with us last evening, it felt like we were his grandchildren, sitting on his farmhouse porch. We are ready to sit on the porch and listen some more, and Charlie will extend our welcome now."

Julia stepped to one side and Charlie moved to the center. "Julia and I both appreciate the honor our youth group has been given to present our speaker. Mr. Campbell did ask us to be brief. But I want to join Julia in saying how much we value the way Dr. Kelly took time to talk with us last evening. Heeding Mr. Campbell's caution to us to be brief, I will just say that all of us in our youth group, and I know all of you, are honored to have a distinguished writer and trusted friend as our guest here at Center Church. So, Julie and I now welcome and present to you, Dr. James Kelly."

While the appreciative applause by the audience was fading, Dr. Kelly stepped forward quickly and said to Julia and Charlie, "Now, wait. Before you leave, I want to ask all in the youth group to stand and be recognized as my newest farmhouse porch grandchildren." During the round of applause that followed, Dr. Kelly cordially shook hands with Julia and Charlie, then turned to the full gathering, and began in his warm and friendly manner.

"Words have power. Words define. I have talked about the Big Ten Universal Qualities we can choose as our brand, our trade mark, our defining image. I have tried to indicate the bigness of the persona these ten words inspire in us, and the good relationships they help us build, but I haven't named them one by one yet, or expanded on their application to daily living. So, let me list them and talk about the Big Ten defining qualities individually. Of course, there will be some overlapping because these qualities are so dynamic as positive identity markers that they cross over into each other.

As I talk about them, it is important to understand the context in which I do all my writing. The focus is on positive identity – not only on who we are in a micro molecular, biological, neurological world, but in a focus on the better story these ten power words can help us write.

Am I qualified to talk about the magnitude of all this by having collaborated with noted authorities who are at the leading edge of science and these qualities? Yes, and no. In personal acquaintances, not as many as I wish. In my reading, the range is wider. Reading is a wonderful medium for connecting with some of the world's greatest thinkers and leading edge philosophers, whom we will never have the privilege of knowing personally. For instance, it's how we get to meet one of Time Magazine's "person of the year," Fabriola Gianotti. She is one of the world's great particle physicists who work with the world's largest machine ever built, the Large Hadron Collider, where she and other scientists are seeking answers to big defining questions about existence. It's exciting to be journeying with the great persons of our progressive story through the connection of reading books and articles.

But, I also have the high privilege of meeting with you, and many other people like you, who are credentialed by your own personal quest to be better persons by putting the Big Ten qualities into real time living in your daily stories right here in your church and community. So, I am privileged to be invited to come and speak to you and share together out of our Big Ten journey of faith.

I write out of my country background. My knowledge base has been extended by three academic degrees, two careers, and lots of reading in science and self-development. I like to think that I am an explorer in the newness of a molecular and neuroscience under-standing of who we are. Even so, I am still in deep water. Some of you have greater expertise than I. It's what I become so aware of as I talk with you informally during break. I respect that highly, and welcome our time together as interdisciplinary explorers. But the question you keep waiting for me to address is, 'What are the Big Ten Universal Qualities - those basic qualities which lead the partnership of science and technology, so linked to an open-ended faith, that they lead us to a new sacred?'

At this highly privileged time, in the long progression of knowledge in the human story, there are ten overarching uni-versal qualities which are so basic and inclusive that they build a framework of identity for our best future as world citizens. This framework of identity has now become a set of word tools we can use to lead us to successful living, in the highest sense of being successful, measured not by fame, wealth, or power, but to how we can be better persons. The first four words are personal qualities, **Kindness, Caring, Honesty,** and **Respect**. The next four are relationship qualities, **Collaboration, Tolerance, Fairness,** and **Integrity,** leading on to the two summit qualities of **Diplomacy, and Nobility.**

These are not religious words. Not legal words. No laws are violated, or even infringed upon wherever they are embraced, anywhere in the world. If they are taught in public centers of in-struction and learning, there is no conflict of interest to defend or protect. They simply define a decent, wholesome life that becomes a sunrise paradigm, calling from the future. They are not rules from yesterday to be protected, but dreams from tomorrow to be treasured. They define a framework for identity based in civiliza-tion's highest and most cherished qualities for common good in our world family.

These ten words need to be incorporated into our mission statements in business, hospitals, political organizations, our media, in our churches, mosques, synagogues, in our universities, and in mediums of lifetime learning and communication. Above all, they need to define an overarching identity framework of who we have the potential to be in our personal story, in this the greatest time in all history!

All ten defining qualities are cousins. These qualities overlap and converge so much that, when they are incorporated into our identity they are kin to each other.

I am always trying to find new and better ways to express them. Maybe cousins is not the best metaphor. Can anyone help me? Nate Harkins, I remember talking to you at one of the Kindness Breakfast Bazaars. You talked about new ways of understanding farming - how, even as it is changing in scale and using new, bigger and better tools, it is still farming, and even if it's vertical farming in our cities, it's still farming. Help me out."

Nate responded thoughtfully. "I am not sure you need much help. I think we understand. We are individuals, but we are also one family where we need to work together beyond our differences, by converging our strengths and the best use of all our resources. In a comparison, little farmers can't make it any more all by themselves. They may still manage one of the little sixty acre farms, but can't make it unless they connect with bigger operations. The little farmers can't afford a drill that costs sixty thousand dollars, or a combine that costs upwards to a half million, so we have to collaborate and work together. I bring in my big machinery to plant his thirty acres of corn and then harvest it in the Fall. And when any farmer contracts for me to come to his farm to harvest the corn, I am in and out in a few hours, thanks to the benefits of technology and engineering in our newest machines. But I couldn't afford that kind of expensive equipment if I didn't contract with almost everyone in the area. We need each other. But, in the end, it's all farming. It all has to fit on a larger scale. What I think you are saying is that, our identity is like that - that we have to think in terms of how everything has to fit together so we can maximize our potential in our time. You are doing just fine. In fact, you make it seem like we are at a big conference on faith, science, and the future."

"Wow, Nate. That's good. I'm glad I asked for your help. You get an "A" for that! In our molecular age, we are increasingly aware of the oneness of all that is, and we have to work with that oneness so that all we do can fit together to enrich all of us. When we get the Big Ten qualities in place in our identity framework they fit together like contract farming. They align us with the oneness of the new sacred.

I want to expand on each of the ten qualities separately, but before I do, I want to put them in historic and philosophical perspective.

The story about Moses, going up to the peaks of Mount Sinai, may have parallels in the stories about the gods meeting with Zeus on Mount Olympus, as in Greek mythology. The story tells about God meeting with Moses there on the peaks of what was considered a sacred mountain. In the story, God did the writing himself. And, yes, he spoke both Egyptian and Hebrew. What? Which language did God write in? Didn't matter. Moses was bilingual, too. I tease about the language. It was the storyteller's way of showing that these ten new guiding laws have a sacred aspect - that they were not just something carried over from Egyptian hierarchical rule and casually put together by the X-Egyptian, Moses. This was a new paradigm of identity that deserved highest respect. The mountain peaks, and laws written on special stones, defined a framework for high expectations. They were a founding "Constitution," a "Bill of Rights" for the future.

The Big Ten Universal Qualities that we list in our time may not have the same metaphorical status with those written on the sacred peaks of Mount Sinai on tablets of stone by the hand of God, but they do have significant credentials and deserve highest respect in defining who we are in our digital-molecular-information age.

They are important qualities, distilled out of all of civilization's long struggle journey and lengthening story. The "big ten" that Moses defined were, time, ethnic, and culture specific. The Big Ten of the new sacred are far more universal and reference our strategic time in shaping our story and our future. They define a higher humanity that crosses over old boundaries, set by yesterdays paradigms, and become a new paradigm call from tomorrow! They align with human dynamics, as defined by the faiths, philosophies, and psychology in our long human experiment up to our digital molecular age. They help us to see things, not so much by how they have been, as by how they can be for a better tomorrow. They set higher aspirations where quality of life will increasingly be even more important than the advances of the tools of science and technology. They extend beyond the continuous rearranging of the power units of social and political control. They respect the long progression in the human story where the potential to reach up for new levels of fulfillment has never been greater.

What I think is that we would be wise to take a mini break, to stand for five minutes and visit with persons nearby before we go on. So, let's take a few minutes break before we look together at the four personal qualities of the Big Ten.

CHAPTER FIVE

The Big Ten
Personal Qualities

Kindness is the quality above all others,
that makes us feel good about ourselves.

LET'S LOOK AT THE FOUR PERSONAL QUALITIES WE CAN CHOOSE TO develop and shape our best tomorrows. The marvel is that while we are trying to make these real in our own story we get the positive feedback benefit right while we are trying to make them our identity markers.

KINDNESS

In our fast-paced, high tech age, when technology is everywhere and drives so much of life, it is more important than ever to make the human quality of kindness our chosen and cultivated persona and trade mark, our brand, our working daily identity markers. Day by day, we all meet so many people who need to receive kindness. But the other side of the coin is that, as much as they need to receive kindness from us, we need ever so much to give kindness to others! The two-way need for kindness is very important for our digital-information-molecular age.

Kindness is the quality above all others, that makes us feel good about ourselves, oils the wheels of human diplomacy, and multiplies our capacity to enjoy life. Anyone who walks around each day with a frozen manikin-look, without the energizing smile of kindness, is working to his or her own disadvantage. Just by being kind to people, we can put a smile on our face that energizes our whole personality for a more successful life.

It's like Edwin Markham says, "There is a oneness that makes us brothers. None goes his way alone. All that we send into the life of others comes back into our own."[8]

Kindness is that quality that lifts each of the other qualities to new and higher levels. People respond to us better when we project kindness. But we have to be genuine about it. If our kindness is merely a façade we put on for advancing self interest, that makes us phonies, and other people will see right through it. What's worse, we will know when we are being disingenuous and will feel less confident and authentic.

But kindness can be real. All day long, we can live in its radiance ourselves, and make it our way of enriching others. It follows, that in order to get what we need from life, we need to help others find what they need. Kindness does that.

When I heard that you are planning a new drama ministry, staged here in this great conference center, as an extension and expansion of your kindness ministry, I was interested and inquired further. I have learned that you are developing plans to begin a dinner theater program here to put on some wholesome plays which build on your local talent base, with the overarching objective of making it into a medium to express kindness and caring to everyone involved in the production, as well as those who come to see the plays. In that sense, it is an extension of your Breakfast

---

[8]   Edwin Markham. "A Creed"

Bazaar. While it will pay for itself financially with gate tickets and some endowment funds, beyond that, it will pay big dividends in kindness. The generosity of one of the talented members of this church, who plans to share her theater experience gratis, is a special kind of ministry and a stewardship of her talent base. I could rightfully ask that person to stand and be recognized, but I know recognition is not at all the name of the game she is playing. It's the kindness game. Far down the years, there may be some who look back on some part they played in a play, but realize the more important part wasn't necessarily on stage, but was the kindness and respect overarching the whole production. It fits in with the mission of your church to be authentic, to be engaged in what you call friendship ministry.

Will people come? They will, especially parents if their children are in the productions. Just as I come out here twice a year for your Kindness Bazaar, guess who will be here for your plays. All any of us ever get is a place in the story, and I want to have a part in that story. So, I'll be here each time.

And when I walk through the corridors of your facilities, which you have now expanded into a tremendous conference and learning center, I note another important ministry that releases the creative side of yourselves through the talents expressed in art. I see the marvelous displays of paintings and pictures people have created and displayed. That is not only a ministry of shared creative insights, but caring and friendship. They help make this a center for kindness and caring.

And you have other important talent sharing ministry. I have learned that the flowers you have in the sanctuary on Sunday, placed in honor or memory of someone, are divided up into four or five smaller arrangements and taken out to people who are not able to attend many functions. It becomes a channel for kindness, not only for the ones receiving the flowers and the visit, but for those who make the visit. The flowers won't last very long, but the memories and kindness will. Half the people in this church are a part of this ministry. The secondary benefit is that you come to know your neighbors and friends, some of whom are fellow members and some who are not. What we know is that kindness goes a long way. It's no wonder I feel such a sense of exhilarating uplift when I come out here.

Will the world be better for this, that we have joined the millions who are doing what they can, in their place in the world's unique settings to make tomorrow better than yesterday? Yes! And will we be better off? Indeed! Kindness carries its own positive rewards! In spite of all the stories of the bad we hear about on the worldwide twenty-four-seven news, kindness can be the story each of us adds, in our own way, to create a better world.

CARING

Kindness and caring go together so much that they are often more than cousins - they are like brothers and sisters, complimenting each other in a reach for outgoing helpfulness.

Caring is consideration of others. Caring sometimes involves making personal sacrifices, but it does not impoverish those who do the caring. On the contrary, some of the "richest" people you will ever know, are the ones who are enriched by their caring. Beyond the benefits that accrue to your life, your story will give the world one more example of how to live the healthy and wholesome life.

Caring does not deplete us. It awakens positive energy. Just thinking how we can care, heals something inside. Let me cite an anonymous example. You don't know her, but you may know people like her. She is a nurse by profession. She bubbles with enthusiasm. Effervescence is in her body language. In two minutes, a stranger could guess what her philosophy of life is. She visits and sends cards to sick people, participates in her church and community by helping out in fund raising projects, invites friends over for dinner, expands hospitality, on and on. It's who she is as a choice. You've known people like her, and needless to say, you admire them. They are big heroes, on whatever size stage. They never sound their own trumpet, and care little whether or not anybody else sounds it. Without fanfare, they will still be who they are - people who are energized and enriched by caring.

Caring can be easy. Caring can be tough. It can be for brief moments. It can extend for years and years. It can require little. It can require so very much. Life is easy for some. Life can be very difficult for others. Wealth comes easy for some. Poverty and struggle beset the pathway for others. But caring people can be found reaching across all these differences.

Life has many stages on which the drama of caring can be played out. You have heard of the ceremony of washing the feet of others as a religious ritual to show humility and caring. But some caring people render even more humility and generous services in their various careers, without ritual, and often without any special thanks or recognition. In fact one of the major ways we can show caring is through our careers. I think of nurses and doctors, of politicians, of business and career leaders, of caregivers at nursing homes, and endearing acts of caring in the home with family - there are so many situations where we find great stories of caring. No titles of praise are given. No badges are pinned or worn. They just earn the silent, respectful title of being people who really care. It's one of the highest titles in anyone's story. People who care are among the world's rich people.

Some of the stories Jesus told about caring will never go out of date. One story was about a man who had been wounded and robbed, and left helpless by the side of the road. Two men saw him lying there, but passed on by without helping. But one man stopped to help, and then took him to an inn and paid the innkeeper to take care of him until he could get back from his journey. The story embodies three philosophies of life. The robber's philosophy of, what's yours is mine and I'll take it. The men who passed on by with a philosophy of, what's mine is mine and I'll keep it. The man who stopped to help lived by an identity of, what's mine is ours and I'll share it. He was the hero in the story.

In our time, multiple foundations are funding caring enterprises on a major scale that only a few years ago seemed impossible. Many business and financial institutions are reshaping their operations in ways that show that they care about what happens to the world family and environment. Research firms, public and private, are expanding our knowledge base and technical skills that define new ways to care. And the collective linkage of humanitarian goodness is helping us to be involved in the causes that overarch religion, culture, and politics to define and work for personal and collective common good. Some share and care out of their talent base, social position, capital resources, and careers, but sometimes it's just many little expressions of the bigness of their heart. These are among the world's greatest heroes.

HONESTY

Honesty is being authentic. Open. No masks. It's being who we really are. "To thine own self be true," said Shakespeare. Easy? Not at all. What is easy is, to put on a false face, spin the story, and pretend to be more important than we really are. There are, however, people who are for real, and who don't hide behind some facade. And when we meet them, we like them. We may even admire them for their open honesty and, in turn, we may aspire to be more open and honest ourselves.

Honesty is one of the more difficult qualities to build into our story. On the other hand, dishonesty is sneaky and can slip up on us in a moment's time when we attempt to protect our delicate, fragile ego, and pride. It's so easy to hide behind spin. It's so easy to blame someone else and excuse ourselves. It's so easy to criticize others when, at the same time we could have been saying something complimentary. But, when we are honest and transparent, we are more open, and less defensive, less intent on hiding our real selves - we can just be ourselves, unpretentious and honest. We don't require of ourselves that we be perfect - just reaching for our best. We can be honest about our inadequacies and mistakes, even laugh at our own blunders.

Some people, who have made big mistakes and done harm to others, change course and go on beyond that to make significant contributions to the human story in spite of their blunders, wrongs, and failures. They turn old endings into new beginnings. It takes a measure of confidence and open honesty just to be who we really are, laugh about ourselves for our failures, but then go on to be bigger than we could ever have been without having to get up and go again beyond failure. That's success!

One more word before we take a full break.

RESPECT

Respect begins with self respect. Talk to yourself. Ask yourself if you were somebody else looking at yourself, would you respect the person you saw? If you say, no, the next question would be to ask, "How can I change that?"

Respect has to do with being held in high regard. By others? Yes. But especially by your own self. It's a worthy goal, but it is not all that easy. To have and hold respect, one has to be true to high expectations. One way to set and reach for those high expectations is to choose the Big Ten Universal Qualities as the identity markers by which you define who you are, and measure by. That's when you will find this fourth marker to be a turning point marker.

I've known a lot of admirable and highly respected people. But, I have also known some who are despicable, who, as in the story of Little Red Ridding Hood, are wolves dressed up as "grandmother" in disguise. Most of the people I have known across the years have earned my respect, but some are "wolves" in attempted disguise. Some pose as being very religious, and get passed off as that, until they do something that shows them up for who they really are. They blow their own cover and loose respect.

But, of course, we are not perfect either, and we know it. Let me clear the air a bit so you will not think you have to be perfect to be respected. Nobody is that perfect. Somewhere, at some time, all of us have betrayed someone's respect for us, or betrayed our own respect. We would be embarrassed for others to know some of the things we keep hidden. We can feel bad about those things years and years later. Respect is an awfully big word to live up to. But we can try, and keep on trying. And when it shows up in our story, it can be something we have earned. To be respected, we have to treat people with respect to earn their trust and confidence. We must do the same for ourselves.

Can we really rebuild and regain respect beyond our failures? The answer is, yes. That has been one of the dominant themes of the Christian faith, that we can begin again, even at the lowest points in our lives, and climb back up. It's a kind of conversion. Old endings can be turned into new beginnings. People can and do reshape their story.

Some of the tools we need in our time are not tools of technology so much as the word tools that give us the energy and inspiration to live by relinquished dreams - words like persistence, renewal, restoration, courage to try again, rebounding, overcoming, re-imaging, reprogramming - positive chosen words that help us to enter a new request of life and keep building a healthy self respect. None of us ever climb a straight line to success, so all of us may need to use the words that help us reset our expectations. To win the true respect of others, we must win and hold respect for ourselves by giving our best to life in successive new beginning points. That's the test all of us must pass if we are to be honored in the wise man's hall of fame.

While it may seem like living by these qualities is easy, it isn't. It's measuring by a demanding standard of excellence that makes it essential to discipline our own story. We reach for our own Olympic gold. We train and retrain the mind and personality until we reach, not perfection, but new levels of respect. And it's all our own responsibility. That's the Solomon thesis. The future we want is up to us. The high respect we plan to give to life becomes our request of life. That is the new sacred.

I think of two persons of high respect who lived without

getting the recognition they deserved for their faithful caring across many years. In their young days, they were in love, just like so many young couples. After they were married, there were several children, and then one special child. He was severely handicapped, physically and mentally. He grew into a man, acutely crippled and having to be cared for like a baby. For forty-seven years, those devoted parents made whatever sacrifices were necessary to give him a home and the best care they could give, before he died. It was extended caring. They earned my respect. And they earned the admiration of others who also walk on tough and challenging un-chosen journeys. They were a living example of caring. They were my grandparents who cared for their special needs son. One of life's highest honors is to be someone who quietly earns that kind of respect.

And, yes, it's time for me to respect the clock that keeps on moving, even when I get caught up in talking about the positive benefits of living by the Big Ten Universal Qualities. So, let's take a break, but during that time feel free to come up and talk with me about ideas that are of interest to you."

CHAPTER SIX

The Big Ten
Relationship Qualities

"It's not the style of clothes one wears, neither the kind of
Automobile one drives, not the amount of money one has in the
bank, that counts. These mean nothing. It is simple service that counts.
--- George Washington Carver

HOLDING UP A SMALL PLATE OF COOKIES, DR. KELLY BEGAN THE SES-
sion saying, "During the break, Amanda, one of the teenage girls
in the youth group came to me bringing a plate of cookies, saying
they were for me to take home with me. When I asked, 'who sent
them?' so I could thank him or her, she said that if she were asked,
'who sent them?' she was to say, 'they are from Anonymous.' So,
maybe Anonymous is here. So, let me begin this second session by
saying, 'Thank you, Anonymous!'

The first four of the big ten identity qualities are focused more
on who we are personally, **Kindness, Caring, Honesty,** and
Respect. The next four qualities have more to do with who we
are in our relationships with others. **Collaboration, Tolerance,**
Fairness, and **Integrity.**

COLLABORATION

Just as kindness is the centerpiece of the four personal qualities, so collaboration leads the four relationship qualities.

Collaboration has always had some part in civilization's story, but some of civilization's best word tools for good relationships have come together now in our age of collective perspective as growing potential. We now have the best conceptual framework and communication word tools the human family has ever had to dream, plan, and work together to achieve a new level of common good. Now that we live as a globally networked society, it is more important than ever to use the new word tools of the Big Ten Universal Qualities to enhance our collective intelligence beyond all boundaries. As an overarching paradigm of oneness, whatever our particular religion, Christian, Jewish, Buddhist, Muslin, or one of many others, we can work together to achieve a greater common good. That framework for a knowledge-based faith is a part of the new sacred.

The Big Ten Universal Qualities are of major importance for our time in history. I teach a Sunday School class where I try to lead those sessions as units where we think together as collaborators on building a better future. We sit in a circle and share openly as colleagues. I like that. These are my young friends and fellow collaborators. We are networking to turn information into knowledge, insight, and wisdom as identity markers for a self-chosen and wiser future.

I like young people and young adults. I enjoy speaking at youth rallies and to college classes. Today's youth and young adults are the ones who need most to learn the Big Ten Universal Qualities, and in turn, teach children to choose them as positive expectations for their best futures. Together we can become one with the daring venture spirit of Eve, and collaborate to think beyond what is, to what can be because we dare to envision new and better tomorrows beyond old yesterdays.

Our best education, then, even when it looks at the past, must always be about the future. And so for our best collaboration – it will be a search for ways we can work together, not to debate the past, but to energize the future we can build together. Instead of building a fortress to defend the old, we can build a launch pad to explore the new. While learning from the past is important, learning from the future is even more important. Collaborating to plan for our best future is sacred.

There is so much that needs our attention and best thinking in our time – climate change, high tech weapons of warfare, disparity between health and disease, the gap between poverty and plenty, the growing gap between fossil based energy and renewable sources of energy, population in balance with earth resources, choosing a lifestyle that makes wholesome use of emerging technology – all these make it increasingly important that we make our age into the age of collaboration in search of a new oneness for the greater good for a world family. It is part of the moral obligation which comes, not from yesterday's restrictions, but from the progression of knowledge and the guidance we can get from working together to make tomorrow better than yesterday. It is a call from the future across all boundaries. In America we sing, "This is my country, land that I love." But it's also time to sing, "This is our planet, land that we love." And beyond that, as the planet's family, it is time to sing, "This is our human family, people with whom we work together." It's time to sing, "We are the World." Collaboration to give our best dreams their best chance to happen has never been more important. It's the new sacred.

All of us collaborate, some in big business contracts, some in scientific inquiry, others in government, in education, but most of us do it in daily connections and relationships, at home, work, and careers without notice. Many great stories of collaboration are evident in modern hospitals. We see examples of collaboration when surgeons work with advanced technology, and with teams of skilled people, to save lives and rebuild health, day after day. Supporting all this, it is important to collaborate to make those medications, devises, and technical tools needed to help create modern marvels. So much of what is sacred is not so much in our worship, as in the dynamic interchanges of our careers and daily activities. It's a synthesis of our converging ability to shape the future on the better side of our cooperative enterprises as a world family.

Collaboration is a necessary part of a good marriage. Incidentally, I have heard that a good marriage is fifty-fifty. Fifty for him, and fifty for him. Of course, the gender in that little story can be turned around. Depends on how much you are willing to laugh at yourself.

In some cohesive and balanced marriages, collaboration is a relaxed, easy relationship, with neither partner's ego threatened. But, in other marriage relationships, couples have to work at getting beyond a constant contest for one to be more right than the other, even battle to be the one who is right all the time. In that dysfunctional contest, collaboration not only breaks down, but war erupts over the least little thing. What the debate is about doesn't matter all that much, it's the fragile ego with its excessive demand to be the one who is right, or at least, not be shown to be wrong, that becomes a battle zone. But it doesn't have to be that way. Conflicts can be defused. The contest loses its storm and furry when at least one person in a relationship brings along even a few of the Big Ten qualities as part of the identity mix, especially kindness, tolerance, fairness, and a willingness to collaborate.

This self-chosen criteria for relationships is not easy, and sometimes we get almost to our wits end when we are working with obstinate people who are too weak to bend and be flexible, or if we are that person. That's when we need people who go the second mile. We may be the one who needs to put on walking shoes and go that extra mile in a reach for larger common good. Collaboration becomes, not the other person's responsibility, but ours. A better tomorrow is ahead when all of us learn how to be one who walks - who reaches out to work together!

In collaboration, the continuing goal is to move the process forward beyond confrontation, whether it be in personal, business, social, or world-community contacts. Wherever we interact with others, we can help move all our relationships to a higher level through the art of collaboration.

More and more now, our collaboration is about our connectedness where we choose the proverbs of collaboration. The Proverbs of Solomon were lost for two hundred years until they were rediscovered for their importance by King Hezekiah. Then, in a metaphorical sense, they got lost again until they were rediscovered by Jesus who became the Teacher who said, "Blessed are the peacemakers." Then they got lost again behind orthodoxy and the systematic theology of transcendence, where having the "right" beliefs became more important than building the right ways to work together for a larger good. Now they are being rediscovered anew in the Big Ten Universal Qualities where the emphasis is on entering our best qualities into working together to make us worthy of our time and place in the progression of the human story. Collaboration to make ours the best story in all history is an essential part of the new sacred.

TOLERANCE

Tolerance is bigness of mind and spirit in relationships.

Sometimes we know what tolerance is by seeing what it isn't when we deal with inflexible, obstinate people. Intolerant people are unbending, inconsiderate, defensive, protective, impatient, without regard for the ideas or feelings of others. Of course, it is all too easy to be one of those persons.

Tolerance is about openness. Religion ought to make people more open and tolerant. Too often it does the opposite. Religion can build rigid walls quickly, that last for days, weeks, years, even centuries. Often, religious people think that because they are protecting old sacred ideas, they are therefore more right than others, when in reality, their rigid defense of old positions is so intense that it actually betrays the highest ideals of any religion.

Tolerance is a big word in the long sweep of history. In 1945 the world came to a turning-point-moment and the United Nations was created. We had seen enough of war and destruction. It was time to give ourselves a new chance. So the Charter of the United Nations says,

> We the people of the United Nations determine to save succeeding generations from the scourge of war, which twice in our lifetime has brought untold sorrows to mankind, and to reaffirm faith in fundamental human rights, in the dignity and worth of the human person, in the equal right of men and women and of nations large and small.... And to these ends, to practice tolerance and live together in peace with one another as good neighbors.[9]

The human family needs a new era of tolerance - flexibility to move forward instead of repeating yesterday - ideological space to dream ahead to define a new level of oneness. It's turning point time! It's time to keep our thinking open. It's time to celebrate our dreams in which, as Solomon said, "the intelligent man is always open to new ideas. In fact he looks for them." Proverbs 8:15.

Real tolerance is about the future, not the past. Tolerance is not just a reluctant agreement on differences; it is the release of energized ideas which make our differences pale in comparison to what we can achieve when we address the better dreams of our human story. Tolerance is about finding a collective unity for our larger common good. It's about defining who we as world citizens. It's about a new era of oneness.

---

[9]   Preamble. The United Nations Charter

FAIRNESS

It has been said many times, "Life is not fair." It's true. The world is not fair. That's just the way it is. The playing field is just not level. Some people have it harder than others, and some people have it very hard, and endure extreme struggle and injustice. That's just the reality of life. Life is not fair.

However, there are people in the world who do their best to make life fairer. Some people are deeply involved in service organizations where the end goal is to make life fairer. They do pancake breakfasts, and barbecue chicken dinners to raise money so they can use it to help others. And, of course, in the process, there is lots of fun and fellowship.

Some persons have created their own channels of caring, helpfulness, consideration, and kindness to make life fairer. These are some of life's great heroes, and the people we admire most.

Some of our heroes have given their lives to help balance the scale of fairness, and are buried in Arlington National Cemetery. Some are buried on hillside cemeteries of small churches, in local villages, and in memorial gardens around the world. And some heroes are living now, just down the road or street, where, day by day, they are carrying out deeds of kindness and compassion without fanfare or recognition. The world owes so much to them and needs them.

Fairness is a measure by which some of the world's hurts are healed and wrongs turned into right, one action at a time. It does not change the destructive unfairness which results from nature's fury in hurricanes, tornadoes, and earthquakes. It does not take away the unfairness that happens to crippled children, abused teenagers, or disadvantaged adults. Even so, there are many people who do what they can to live by the quality of fairness in an unfair outside Eden world.

There is more fairness in the world now. Yes, that can be debated, because there are such glaring instances where unfairness is evident. On the other hand, there are so many instances in which fairness has increased significantly. Much credit for that goes to the increase in knowledge and its dissemination through digital communication and advances in technology. Scientific research is increasing our ability to address unfairness in our world – unfairness like when children died fifty years ago for lack of modern medical equipment and pharmaceuticals, unfairness which leaves children without knowing how to read, unfairness which leaves some cultures far behind in the benefits of technology. In the progression of the human story we can work in many ways to close the unfairness gaps.

Major foundations are helping the world family have access to advanced medical help. Teachers in networks of learning centers around the world have reversed much of the reading gap and digital knowledge divide. Major foundations are extending the benefits of healing medications in some of the most critical areas of the world. Goodwill missions of churches and clubs have dug wells and made clean drinking water available instead of disease ridden water from rivers. Business and industrial organizations are lending their expertise to help solve problems across cultural divides. Organizations of goodwill and social service are adding significantly to the sacrificial effort to help heal the hurting side of humanity. There is still so far to go, but it's a great story and one that needs to be celebrated.

We may write our own best story when we choose to give our best to help make the world fairer. We dare not wait for the world around us to be fair before we give dreams their best chance to happen in our own success story where we turn hardship and struggle into opportunity to write a winning story in spite of unfairness. We can be one of those who turn unfairness around. It is as President Barack Obama has said, "we have a stake in each other's success."[10]

But, now a big question is arising. Are we increasing fairness in our link with Mother Nature? Does Mother nature think we are being fair?

It has to do with the next relationship quality, integrity.

---

[10]   Barack Obama. *The Audacity of Hope.*

INTEGRITY

Integrity has to do with the honorable uses we make of civilization's gifts which have been created slowly on the long journey of struggle, up to our time and place in the story. It has to do with our relationship to the amazing gifts of nature we are accessing in new ways in our molecular-digital age. Integrity has to do with making sure the high expectations we hold for other people, are the same ones we require of ourselves. In the same sense, what we expect of the gifts of nature, nature then has a right to expect of us in return, that we use its gifts wisely. What is becoming a collective bargain, is that if we shortchange nature, it will, out of its very nature, shortchange us. This new quid pro quo gives us the responsibility to learn more about nature, and the interrelated molecular nature of all existence as part of the new sacred.

It's time for a new level of honesty in the way we live. Even if our scientists are only seventy-five percent correct in their assessment that we are making more demands on nature than it can supply, this new knowledge makes it imperative that we make the ways we live an essential stewardship of who we are trying to be in our place in the big world citizen, molecular age story.

If we link integrity with wisdom, we will carefully balance the number of people we add to the human family, and its drain on what nature can supply. That linkage comes as a call from the future to chose a wise balance, and to do so in a long-term understanding of our place in the story. Can we be trusted to do our part? Can religion be trusted to see this call from the future as a vital part of the new sacred?

Science must have integrity. Findings in science must be trustworthy, repeatable, and verifiable. No quackery is permissible. Shouldn't religion have parallel criteria for credibility? Shouldn't the assumptions and paradigms in religion be re-examined as the progression of our human story moves forward? Integrity in our faith is as important as it is science. It is an essential part of the new sacred.

CHAPTER SEVEN

The Big Ten
Summit Qualities

Noblesse oblige. Nobility obligates.

BEYOND THE **PERSONAL QUALITIES** AND THE **RELATIONSHIP QUALI-ties** there are the **summit qualities** of diplomacy and nobility.

DIPLOMACY

What is it? What does it do? How can we build it? And, who wants to be a diplomat?

What is it? Webster's Dictionary defines diplomacy as "skill in handling affairs without arousing hostility." No need to rub the cat's fur the wrong way. The cat doesn't like it. Diplomacy can be our chosen way of making relationships more workable and pleasant. It's a matter of being cooperative, even in tough negotiations. A diplomat does not work against others, but with them, and even for them, as well as for his or her own interests.

What does diplomacy do? Diplomacy builds mutual respect for more positive relationships. It multiplies friends. Increases joy. Advances career success. Increases good health. Makes life more fun.

Good diplomacy has to do with being outgoing and caring enough to lift human relationships to a level of flexibility in making agreements and effective plans. Diplomacy smoothes life's rough edges. There is no need to go through life trying to push our weight around in selfish demands that others must meet us on our terms. It can, and does, backfire and results in defensive resistance. Diplomacy is not twisting arms, or bending attitudes. It's not spin. It's not manipulation of relationships only to one's own advantage. On the contrary, diplomacy is working together for larger mutual benefits.

Diplomacy can be tricky. If we don't give other people room to be at least somewhat right, they won't give us room either. Resistance takes over and egos can be very defensive and hold rigid positions. The "billy goat" effect kicks in. If you are trying to get a goat to go where it doesn't want to go it locks its four feet in reverse and you succeed only if you drag it. Diplomacy is giving room for both sides to agree without one threatening the other into dead-lock. Diplomats reach for flexibility and compatibility. Everybody gets to win something. Diplomacy is finding a way two old goats can find some reason to move forward with advantage.

How can we build it? Diplomacy is where the Big Ten qualities compliment each other. Kindness builds diplomacy. Fairness is the "modus operandi" of diplomacy. Collaboration advances diplomacy as a means of sharing many ideas and working together. We build diplomacy when we decide we want to be a person others enjoy being around and working with. It is a chosen quality and can be learned by practice, day by day, in multiple relationships at home, school, work, socialization, play, and especially between marriage partners.

Words are tools. Diplomatic words change attitudes in an exchange of ideas. We build diplomacy by choosing our words carefully, wisely, and in a bigger context where the goal is understanding and cooperation.

Who wants to be a diplomat? Diplomats are those who

want to reach for the upper levels of compatible agreements. Who, then wants to be a diplomat? All of us who want to make life more pleasant and fun for others, and much more fun for ourselves. There's nothing wrong with wanting to be a pleasant person others like to work with and be around. In fact, it is wise.

Diplomacy deals with end results of all our relationships, whether in major transactions of business, social policy, government agreements, or in little daily negotiations at home, school, office, party events, marriage - wherever we interact in give-and-take relationships with others. A diplomat is always trying to build good working relationships for good outcomes. Interactions may be brief, and our words few, but being a diplomat is still one of the leading ways to reach worthy objectives.

Diplomacy is a gracious way of living out a high humanity in each little relationship. Easy? We know it isn't. It is a learned skill. Sometimes we have to learn the hard way, over and over again, until we finally get it, and grow in our ability to be diplomatic. It is a working part of the new sacred.

Now for the summit word.

NOBILITY

We have heard this phrase many times, *noblesse oblige*. Nobility obligates. It has reference to being honorable, responsible, and generous by reason of high rank or birth. High rank or birth - "that's us!" We have been born to high privilege in the digital-information-molecular age. No other generation, in all the human story has ever been born to so many benefits, or with so great a launch pad for liftoff into this new age of unfinished dreams as we have in our digital-information-molecular age.

All the way from the cave man to the moon landing astronauts, civilization's inchworm developments have increased our potential to achieve big dreams so that we owe far more to the future than ever before. Nobility obligates us proportionate to our privilege, as the Master Teacher said, "To whom much is given, of him shall much be required." We have more than an obligation; we have a tremendous opportunity to make the Big Ten Universal Qualities the markers that guide us to success.

Ten words. Ten power words. Anyone who chooses these ten words for his or her identity markers will be a better person. These words will awaken "the better angels of our nature."

Do I achieve my goals? Sometimes, yes. Sometimes, no. But when it's No, that is when yesterday's failures become today's teachers. Our failures may even be the only things that finally get our attention enough to make us ready to listen. Over time, the reach for the Big Ten qualities will reprogram our mind and identity in which our privileged place in the story becomes a new request of life. Even though it takes time, it does work! Finally, the brain gets it. Something gets healed inside. We become better persons! It's the new sacred!

It may be good if we see these challenges refracted in the words of President Theodore Roosevelt in his speech, "Citizens In A Republic."

> *It is not the critic who counts; not the man who points out how the strong man stumbles, or where the doer of deeds could have done better. The credit belongs to the man who . . . if he fails, at least fails while daring greatly, so that his place shall never be with those cold and timid souls who know neither victory nor defeat.*

Achieving all ten of these big ten qualities may be beyond our grasp, but they must never be beyond our reach. When the story is complete, we can be respected as someone who pushed back the edge of the possible and chose to live on the growing edge of the future!

As we conclude, let me refer to a familiar little poem. It's Eugene Field's poem about a little boy's behavior just before Christmas, in which the little boy says, "Jest 'fore Christmas, I'm as good as I kin be." Why? There was a payoff.

For us, every day is "jest before Christmas" with a payoff in life for being "as good as we can be." What helps us to do this? It's the Big Ten Universal Qualities that become the guiding markers we measure by and live up to. When these qualities define who we are, and what we plan to give to life, they become a request of life with a rewarding payoff.

And, now it's time to say, goodnight. But that doesn't mean we must stop talking. Come around and let's share ideas and stories for as long as you like. I never tire of it.

CHAPTER EIGHT

Dream Your Best Dream!

We are crossing a great divide
from the authority-based religion
over to an open-ended, knowledge-based faith.

DR. KELLY STOOD AT THE CENTER OF THE PLATFORM. AT HIS RE-quest, the speakers lectern had been taken away. He began, speaking with more enthusiasm than usual to an equally enthusiastic young audience. As his opening words, in his open and cordial manner, he said, "After the close of our session last evening, Julia and Charlie were among several of you in your youth groups who came up to talk with me. They asked if there was a way I could devote one session just for young people. Immensely pleased with the idea, I thought for a moment and then said, 'Do you think we could have an early session before the next evening session?' You were enthusiastic in saying, 'We can!' You said you would get on your cell phones and get as many young people here as possible for an early session.

Now, here you are, with a sign on the door outside that says YOUTH SESSION IN PROGRESS. ADULTS PLEASE WAIT. However you did it, you did it! I haven't counted but there must be forty to fifty of you here. When I asked if there were questions I should address, Julie said, 'Could you talk to us like a grandfather, like we are sitting on your farmhouse porch?' I was greatly honored by that request! It was like 'going platinum.' So here we go, 'my newest grandchildren!'

You have a unique opportunity in your time in history to define your best future by taking command of your greatest power – your power to choose your thoughts. Each of you has that power. It's in the DNA you have inherited – the power to think and turn your thoughts into signals to your brain and then from your brain into choices.

Jessie B Rittenhouse wrote a poem which can be an important metaphor for you.

> I bargained with Life for a penny,
>   And Life would pay me no more,
> However I begged at evening
>   When I counted my scanty store.
>
> For Life is a just employer,
>   He gives you what you ask,
> But once you have set the wages,
>   Why, you must bear the task.
>
> I worked for a menial's hire,
>   Only to learn, dismayed,
> That any wage I had asked of Life,
>   Life would have willingly paid. [11]

You need not bargain with Life for a penny. You are worth more than that – much more! In fact, you are worth all you tell yourself you are worth.

---

[11] Ibid.

I want to talk about your self-chosen identity in your time, in what is sometimes labeled as the cell-phone age.

There are many people who are more ready to defend yesterday than there are who define tomorrow. That is most unfortunate. I want to encourage you to define tomorrow. You have an opportunity to reach beyond just advancing the techno-humans that all of us are becoming in our wonderful time in history. You have an opportunity to be among the exceptional people. So, as I talk to you, I want to ask you to dream your best dream!

To help you do that, I want to talk about an open-ended faith and the new sacred.

You will see more change by the time you finish college a few years from now than I have seen in my lifetime. You may even be able to live much longer than I. Your place in the story will increasingly be defined digitally, where you learn, work, and relate to others by way of digital technology, without reference to place and time. With your cell phone, laptop, iPad, and their newer versions, you can access the data banks of information instantaneously across all geographical, cultural, religious, and political boundaries. You are growing up with this level of technology and may not fully realize that, unintentionally, you are building a collective knowledge base and global identity. I welcome this. I welcome and celebrate the new information technology you use so easily. But, along with that, you will need something far more important - a simple, basic philosophy of life and self-image that can help you shape your future by a wholesome, creative identity that grows as you grow. You will need a guiding template of qualities that serve your own best interests for as long as you may live, and with whatever new technologies each new generation may create. You will need the Big Ten Universal Qualities.

I want to encase this summary of a wholesome, positive philosophy of life in three very different stories. The first story is about Amos, ancient prophet of Israel. Second, I want to tell the story of Solomon, the writer of a success and self-development book for the young people of his time, the book of *Proverbs*. The third story is about Camp Tekoa, a youth camp, where the contrast between the two major paradigms and philosophies of life represented in my first and second stories is shown in real time.

Amos lived in ancient Tekoa, a small mountain city in southern Israel. He was a dresser of sycamore figs, a fruit eaten by poor people. In order for those figs to be soft enough to eat when they got ripe, they had to be mashed one by one while still on the bushes. Amos did that. But in addition to that, Amos was a shepherd. To sell his sheep he would drive them many miles north of Tekoa.

One year when Amos drove his sheep to market, he became very distraught when he learned about a way of life there. It was a big contrast to the way he lived as a vinedresser and shepherd among poor people. In our vernacular, he was shocked! There he saw the lifestyle of the wealthy merchants who took advantage of the plight of the poor. And when he walked into their places of worship, he couldn't believe what he was seeing – so many statues to various gods other than his one God, Yahweh. And when he learned about the fabulous country homes these people had, and saw how their wealth and elaborate lifestyle were built on the backs of young slaves they had bought from poor parents, he just couldn't keep quiet about the wrongs he saw. He couldn't just sell his sheep then go on back home and continue his simple way of life and say nothing. So, he began to speak out against the abuses he saw all around him while he was there. He put his words into oracles, as though God were speaking through him in anger about the ways they were living and worshipping.

What Amos saw sent his mind into a spin. He watched as the most wealthy people in town came to their temples of worship with their gifts. But Amos did not assume that God was pleased with their gifts, which they gave as showy badges to demonstrate how religious they were. In spite of their gifts, they lacked caring and compassion. They were religious, but not humanitarian. Before they would do any favor for poor people, they demanded bribes, which the poor people just couldn't afford. Soon the poor people got so deep in debt to the rich merchants that they had to sell their own children into slavery just to pay off their debts. In no way did the way of life of these people match what they claimed in their religion. Amos was furious! So furious, in fact, that he began to speak, and, later, to write his oracles.

> Listen, you merchants who rob the poor, trampling on the needy; you who long for the Sabbath to end and the religious holidays to be over, so you can get out and start cheating again - using your weighted scales and under-sized measures; you who make slaves of the poor, buying them for their debt of a piece of silver or a pair of shoes, or selling them your moldy wheat. Amos 8:4-6 TLB

Amos was equally disdainful of their worship. As though he spoke for God, he said,

> I hate your show and pretense - your hypocrisy of 'honoring' me with your religious feasts and solemn assemblies. I will not accept your burnt offerings and thank offerings. I will not look at your offerings of peace. Away with your hymns of praise - they are mere noise to my ears. I will not listen to your music, no matter how lovely it is. Amos 5:21 - 23 TLB

Wow! Amos was fired up.

The idols they displayed in great prominence in their places of worship seemed like betrayal and mockery.

> Go ahead and sacrifice to idols at Bethel and Gilgal. Keep disobeying - your sins are mounting up. Sacrifice

each morning and bring your tithes twice a week! Go
through all your proper forms and give extra offerings.
How you pride yourselves and crow about it everywhere!
Amos 4:4-5 TLB

Amos assumed God had bent over backward for them, but they
had not reciprocated with respect. So now God was angry and
would have to take a different approach. He would now punish
them into submission.

The Lord says, "The people of Israel have sinned again
and again, and I will not forget it. I will not leave them
unpunished any more. For they have perverted justice by
accepting bribes, and sold into slavery the poor who can't
repay their debts; they trade them for a pair of shoes. They
trample the poor in the dust and kick aside the meek.
Amos 2:6-7 TLB

I will destroy the beautiful homes of the wealthy - their
winter mansions and their summer houses, too - and de-
molish their ivory palaces." Amos 3:15 TLB

Amos spoke clearly. But nobody was ready to listen. He had
driven his sheep to market, but that was all they wanted from
him - just his sheep - not his oracles. So, they asked him to leave -
to go back to Tekoa, back to his figs and flocks. So he left, but
he couldn't forget about what he had seen. And he couldn't keep
quiet. Even though he didn't belong to any prophetic order, he
began to write like a prophet, and put his writing into oracles
from God.

Amos was right, but he was also wrong. The outcry of
Amos against injustice was merited. But his concept of how to
correct it was not. He was short sighted and provincial with
very little tolerance for ways to worship that were different. In

his paradigm, God is in charge and everything and people must conform to his ways or else. It was a paradigm of an angry God who would punish people until they conform. It's the thesis of an authority based religion that shows up in most of the religions of mankind, even up to our time as a religion of fear and God's final judgment.

In contrast, the second story is about Solomon. There is a book in the Bible which has a very different view of God from that of Amos. It's the book of *Proverbs*, a collection of proverbs by King Solomon. It's different from any other book in the Bible. In *The Book of Proverbs*, God doesn't straighten out the world, people do. God doesn't micromanage the outcome of history and punish people into compliance. Instead, people make choices which determine their own future. It's their responsibility to look ahead and make wise choices.

Solomon had been appointed to be king by his father, King David, while he was still very young - around twenty-one. He now presided over a vast kingdom reaching from the Tigris and Euphrates Rivers, in what is now Iraq, all the way to the Nile River in Egypt. Young Solomon was overwhelmed by the magnitude of the responsibility. So he went up to the temple at Gilgal and appeared before the altar with this prayer:

"O Lord my God, now you have made me the king instead of my father David, but I am as a little child who doesn't know his way around. And here I am among your own chosen people, a nation so great that there are almost too many people to count. Give me an understanding mind so that I can govern your people well and know the difference between what is right and wrong." I Kings 3:7-9

God was pleased and said, "I'll give you what you asked for! I will give you a wiser mind than anyone else has ever had or ever will have." I Kings 3:12

Solomon's dream may have been mostly a projection of his

own future, but his image of himself as the leader of a better way to live was a defining moment. It was a new paradigm. Instead of a sunset paradigm, that measured by the past, it was a sunrise paradigm, that measured by dreams of a better future. Instead of plunging ahead by violent force, dominance, and control, as his father had done, he envisioned a new tomorrow with his people building a new future through trading and cooperation. It was a choice they could make. By doing wise thinking, they could make a better future than the past. A new kind of hero was coming alive in his mind. He defined the of hero of the successful life in little sayings, known as proverbs.

King Solomon wrote and collected many wise sayings, so young people could have a guiding template for how to make the best decisions in a broken world. So, for young people today, the book of *Proverbs* is one of the best books in the Bible you can read! Here are a few of his proverbs:

These are the proverbs of King Solomon of Israel, David's son:
He wrote them to teach his people how to live -
how to act in every circumstance,
for he wanted them to be understanding, just and fair
in everything they did. Proverbs 1:1-3

A wise youth makes hay while the sun shines, but what a shame
to see a lad who sleeps away his hour of opportunity. Proverbs 10:5

Teach a child to choose the right path.
and when he is older he will remain upon it. Proverbs 22:6

Determination to be wise is the first step
toward becoming wise. Proverbs 4:7

To learn you must want to be taught. Proverbs 12:1

The wise man looks ahead. Proverbs 14:8

*He who loves wisdom loves his own best interest
and will be a success. Proverbs 19:8*

*If you must choose, take a good name rather than great riches;
for to be held in loving esteem is better than silver and gold. Proverbs 22:1*

*The intelligent man is always open to new ideas. In fact, he
looks for them. Proverbs 18:15*

*If you profit from constructive criticism you will be elected
to the wise man's hall of fame. Proverbs 15:31*

So here are two major contrasting paradigms of God. One is the God who is up there somewhere, out beyond the universe. The other is the God who is down here, in and within the universe, a part of all molecular existence. Which paradigm we choose makes a big difference in how we understand who God is, but even more, who we are.

When I was your age, I had been taught and believed in the God of Amos, who was up there. Over the years I have discovered the God of Solomon, who is down here. I have discovered the God of all molecular existence, discoverable by an open-ended faith. It is a faith in which we are learning about our place in the macro universe of stars and galaxies, solar systems and planets. It is a faith in which we are learning about the micro universe of the smallest particles of existence and the behavior of atoms and their interactions. This perspective on the nature of existence is changing the ways any of us can think about God. But even more, it is a story about us - about a faith we can choose for our place in the story. It's the new sacred.

Amos served a God of transcendence - up there.

Solomon serve a God immanence - down here.

Amos served an angry God of judgment who is up there.

Solomon served a God of learning and new tomorrows, who is down here.

Amos represents looking back upon a fixed religion.

Solomon represents looking forward through an open-ended faith and the story we can live.

Amos had an authority-based religion in which the requirements are already set. God dictates all things from afar, up there, far beyond the world. The future is to be informed by the past, already designed and fixed.

Solomon had an open-ended faith. His God was in this world where people are creating their own stories. Solomon set forth multiple proverbs which are little templates of life's finest qualities, to be chosen because they bring better rewards in any person's story. People are responsible for discovering insights and advancing their knowledge so they can be informed for making wise choices.

The two major contrasting paradigms are being played out in different churches in our time, to which you may go and listen, as you try to figure out how things work, and who you are, and who you can to be.

When you go to some churches you will hear the thunder sounds of Amos and his God of judgment, with its authority claim to be the voice of God, scaring you out of your wits in fear of God's punishment. Chicken Little preachers gain popularity, posing as prophets of the future by describing apocalyptic scenarios of doom, using the science fiction and final-days myths from a few books in the Bible, especially the book of Revelation. These modern day prophets put words in God's mouth, just as Amos did, as though they know what God is thinking, and what one must do to meet his demands. The reality is that nobody knows that much about God, then or now.

But in other churches, far more quietly, you can listen in a quest for insight and understanding. You recognize an open-source, knowledge-based faith and hear the quiet whisper of the proverbs of Solomon. You learn to respect the God of new tomorrows by learning more about the macro and micro forces at work in all existence that just keep on "going and going." In that understanding of God, there is great mystery. We marvel at whatever drives the oneness of existence that makes water run down hill, and has continued to run down hill for millions of years. It's an approach of awe and great respect, where we are partners with ongoing creation. It's the new sacred.

We are crossing a great divide from the authority-based religion over to an open- ended, knowledge-based faith. Theological paradigms are giving way to new paradigms that incorporate advances in technology and information into the ways we understand God and define the best way to live.

One case in point is our responsibility for our own earth ecology and environment, informed by new knowledge, created by research using our expanding instruments of knowledge. For instance, through data from satellites encircling our earth, we are learning how our water and land resources are being overrun by the demands from a massive earth population, which is on the verge of becoming a crisis, unless we change the way we live, and make wiser usage of earth resources, and learn more about how to balance world population with that. There is no God watching over the threat of depleting earth resources - that's man's responsibility. The relationship of food supply to human population is a critical factor in defining who we are, but it's not up to God - it's up to us. We are the ones who need to mend the brokenness of our ways and to redefine family and lifestyle so that we can have a stable earth population that is balanced with earth resources. It's our responsibility to work toward a collective common good and a wise future for the earth family. The paradigm shift is from, thinking of God as up there, transcendence, to a paradigm of partnership with a God, down here, immanence, interrelated with all we are learning about the nature of existence and what is happening in our real world.

We are at a new beginning in a golden age of faith. We have the knowledge base to launch us into the age of the new sacred, where the focus is not on our theology, or even our technology, but on our humanology, to coin a new word. Sounds like a good word to me.

All of us go through phases in which the choices we make are identity choices. In the youth phase you are in now, it's easy to feel insecure and measure too much by what other people think. It's easy to think others have a better chance at living a more successful life, have a more popular brand, a better personality, better homes and parents, and are smarter than you. But what is more important than any of that, significant as it may be, is to discover your own unique qualities and strengths, and to make the development of those into a defining and leading-edge self-image that you choose to send to your own brain as a request for its guidance.

Living in a good society can help, but that's not the main story. Having the support of good parents is helpful, but that's not the main story either. Having the best education is very important, but even that is not the main story. The main story is the choices you make where you choose to make the best of what you have and develop that into skills and services as what you plan to give to life.

Many people make a success of life in spite of living in a disadvantaged society. It's not the world around us, it's the dream within us that counts most. It's not the absence of struggle and hardship, but the power of our resolve to overcome them that resets our identity. It's not who our parents are, but who we are, and who we plan to be, that signals the future. It's not living in the house that technology built, it's living as world class citizens in our time and place in the story that makes our story the best we can make it. It's true, as a modern day proverb states, the qualities we plan to give to life become our request of life.

The third story is about Camp Tekoa. It's a good place to think about the God of all existence, and who you are. Camp Tekoa is a little camp, nestled in the mountains of North Carolina. It is more wooded than the small mountains where Amos lived in ancient Tekoa. Here, for one week, young people can have great fun together as they play, sing, dance, and think ahead about their own identity. Even in so brief a time, they can create great dreams that honor their best request of life.

When you first drive into the camp, you go along a narrow gravel road that leads down through the woods to the camp where its buildings are clustered along one side of a little lake, called Lake Susan. Scattered among the trees along the lakeside are cabins for girls, and beyond that, cabins for boys. Then in the week of activities, a cabin of girls and a cabin of boys join together to form a "home in the woods," in a campfire circle, to sing songs, play games, and prepare dinner over an open fire.

Back at camp center, near the parking lot where campers unload from the cars, say goodbye to their parents, and set off to their cabins, is the dining room where campers have their meals. The one or two exceptions to that is when campers carry their food up the trails to their home in the woods, and work together to cook their meal over an open campfire. But here in the rustic main dining room, if you happen to be late for breakfast one morning, all the other campers will sing to you.

Good morning to you.
Good morning to you.
We're all in our places,
With sunshiny faces.
What happened to you?
What happened to you?

You may feel like crawling under the table, but in the spirit of their jesting comradery, you will join the other campers at the table in a supportive fellowship.

Every morning, right after breakfast, each camper is expected to find an isolated spot, out among the trees, or alongside Lake Susan, to sit quietly for fifteen minutes to read and think, in a devotional reflection on one's own identity. Yes, of course, a boy's thoughts may drift away to that nice girl at the breakfast table, or in their campfire circle, and a girl's thoughts may drift away to that cute boy she got to dance with at the evening social. But those energizing ideas can fit into a larger identity in which each young camper, regardless of race, culture, religion, politics, social, or economic categories, builds his or her own infrastructure of guiding, overarching, self images as a personal GPS - their Identity Guidance System. During those early morning reflective moments, as they look out across little Lake Susan, they may realize anew that their best answers will not come from outside so much as from inside. Here is where an inner storyteller can help them dream a dream that honors the best of humanity's dreams for their own best future. And here is where that inner storyteller needs the foundational words of the Big Ten Universal Qualities to inform each camper's personal identity base. Here is where the God of all molecular existence may become real in their life experience as they try to be a person who lives by the personal qualities of Kindness, Caring, Honesty, and Respect, who lives by the relationship qualities of Collaboration, Tolerance, Fairness, and Integrity, who lives by the summit qualities of Diplomacy and Nobility. These are the guiding signals which align their story with an understanding of the God down here.

Some years ago, J B Phillips wrote a book entitled, *Your God Is Too Small.* He wrote that little book before astronauts had set foot on the moon, or astronomers had begun to explore the heavens with the Hubble Telescope to learn about the billions of galaxies, millions of light years apart. That was before physicists had built the

Large Hadron Collidor where they could search for the subatomic particles of molecular existence. It will be most unfortunate if, in this age of the greatest expansion of macro and micro knowledge, with new instruments of inquiry, the human family follows a God that is too small. If we dare to make God so small that we fail to see some kind of new knowledge about God in all that energizes and sustains the oneness of all molecular existence, our God will be too small.

Sometimes the advance in understanding is such a big step, that a major paradigm shift is necessary. The ideas that Solomon put forth were so different from the concepts held by Amos that they embodied a new paradigm, a very different way of looking at life and how one can think about God.

The views of Amos are representative of some parts of the Bible, where God has the whole story of history planned, all the way down to the end, and people are expected to fit into that pre-designed plan or else God will punish them. That view of how the world works scares the wits out of us when we are young, and are just beginning to learn about the nature of existence.

In contrast, and in a far more positive and healthy worldview, the proverbs of Solomon speak of people being accountable for the history they are writing, especially their own personal story. His proverbs ask us to be smart about our own life and to make those choices which are wise and wholesome.

The views of Amos are representative of those in our time who believe in a distant God, much like a super person, with a super data bank, who watches over everything that happens and rewards or punishes people in accordance with how well they obey the rules defined in the ancient writings of the Bible, entrenched traditions, and rigid theology.

In contrast, the views of Solomon are representative of people who believe in the expansion of knowledge and its tools of exploration through science and technology, and who follow a faith that is open-ended and based in growing knowledge, so that successive generations can keep adding new insights which inform the way to live the best life in an ever-changing world.

The Solomon concept of God can is advanced in our time in the paradigm of a partnership of science and faith, and an identity framework which can be defined by ten words as the Big Ten Universal Qualities. This expanding knowledge base makes it important to cross the bridge from an authority-based religion, informed by Amos' kind of thinking, over to a knowledge-based faith, informed by Solomon's kind of thinking. With respect for our past, we can have even more respect the future. It's important to make those choices which give our best dreams their best chance to happen.

Modern psychology is on the side of Solomon. Behavior is learned and set by the identity we accept for ourselves. Instead of defining who we are by sunset paradigms from the past, we can begin to program our minds by the sunrise paradigm with signals from our future and great expectations in the greatest age of potential for a better tomorrow that the world has ever known. That's the age you are a part of. When young persons hang a word picture of the Big Ten Universal Qualities on the walls of their minds, they magnetize their minds to find those key qualities in their own life experiences and developing story.

Young people may try to imagine the good life and think that those who have the latest sports cars, the biggest houses, the most money, go on spring break and expensive vacations to far away resorts, are the ones who have found the good life.

Not so, says Martin Seligman, who was for many years the president of the American Psychological Association, and author of *Authentic Happiness*. He introduced the more dependable premise for modern psychology called, positive psychology. His extensive clinical studies revealed something far different. He asks,

> *What is the good life? In my view, you can find it by following a startlingly simple path. The 'pleasant life' might*

be had by drinking champagne and driving a Porsche, but not the good life. Rather the good life is using your signature strengths every day to produce authentic happiness and abundant gratifications. This is something you can learn to do in each of the main realms of your life: work, love, and raising children. [12]

What I call the Big Ten Universal Qualities, Dr. Seligman calls "signature strengths." He says they take "an act of will," and "with enough time, effort, and determination . . . can be acquired by almost any ordinary person." [13]

Neuroplasticity is on the side of Solomon's proverbs. It is based in the growing reality that the mind can change itself, that it can create an Identity Guidance System. The growing paradigm in neuroscience is that even when the brain is damaged by injury or disease, or has been locked in by negative thinking, the future is still open. Dr. Norman Doidge, in his book entitled, *The Brain That Changes Itself,* has shown that the brain can rebuild its capacity to help people overcome major disabilities. The brain is not hardwired. It can be preprogrammed, programmed, and reprogrammed to give new and helpful guidance. The brain need not be set by the past, but set and reset by our best dreams and future expectations we can enter for ourselves.

Success and self-development philosophy is on the side of Solomon. A dependence on God to bring about solutions to life's challenges is not as healthy as taking responsibility for our own ways to build health and wholeness into our story. The Solomon thesis of "it's up to you," opens a pathway to self-reliance, self-confidence, and personal initiative. It becomes a contest within ourselves. Instead of being passive and hoping that chance, or other people, will solve life's problems for us, the winning contestant

---

[12]   Martin E P Seligman. *Authentic Happiness* p 13

[13]   Ibid. p 135

becomes pro-active and makes choices and plans to build one's own best future. One summary is in the cliché, "God helps those who help themselves." There is no savior waiting to rescue us. We are the ones who can choose to put the Big Ten Universal Qualities into the dynamics of our own story. It's up to us. It's the new sacred.

It was Abraham Maslow who gave us the pyramid of values with its assertion that we have to meet the most basic need for safety and security before we can climb up to other values. What I want you to do is to go ahead and put in a claim on life that is bigger than just safety and security. What we know is that we can be choosers - that safety and security need not limit who we are trying to be - that our DNA gives us the capacity to intentionally choose the higher and less self-centered values, even spend a lifetime in which we define our future by the markers of the Big Ten Universal Qualities. If you reach for your best tomorrow beyond just being secure, you will be reaching for a far more rewarding life! Having noble dreams and challenging goals will bring out your best and make you a part of a winners game!

Why not go ahead and set high expectations?

Why not reach for some worthy causes bigger than your security? Why not reach for that summit of the universal qualities, for nobility? Why not reach for what Lincoln called, "the better angels of our nature?"

Why not move beyond fear and reach for a tomorrow of courage and confidence and take a chance on our best dreams? After all, it's as Bette Midler sings in Amanda McBroom's words, "It's the dream, afraid of waking that never takes the chance."

Why not sing with Louis Armstrong, "It's a wonderful world?"

Why not sing "Every time it rains, it rains Pennies from heaven?"

Why not trade in your sunset paradigm for a new sunrise paradigm?

Let this, then, be the story you write - a story where the good you plan to give to life becomes your request of life – where you give your best dreams their best chance to happen!

So what, you don't have some advantages you assume other kids around you have, make the most of what you have. So what, your parents don't have money and fame, or even if they do, you can set a course for yourself, defined by your own winning plans and dreams. If you don't have the brain power to make top grades, you can do the best you can with the abilities you have, without excusing yourself because someone else makes better grades. You can refuse to let your aspirations be defined by your limitations. You can develop your potential to its maximum in ways that are unique and special to you. You can be authentically you. Give the best you can to life, as your request of life.

Beginning now, with your own personal story, you can make your story a success story. If you make the Big Ten Universal Qualities a template that you overlay on your plans, they become a vital part of your noble request of life. The world doesn't have to be just right before you try your best. You can be a change agent for a better tomorrow. You can follow the call of Mahatmas Gandhi, 'be the change you want to see in the world.'

What then, are those big qualities we need for success?

Mike Krzyzewski is known as the highly successful basketball coach at Duke University, across more than three decades. He is also recognized for his continuing emphasis on nine principles that define the best of Duke athletics. They are: education, respect, integrity, diversity, sportsmanship, commitment, loyalty, accountability, and excellence. In a close parallel to these, there are the Big Ten Universal Qualities you can choose that will help you to be winners. These are the qualities that add to the best of civilization's continuing best qualities and a credit to your name and story!

Is it easy to learn the ten words? Yes. Anyone can do that. Is it easy to actually make these qualities define who you are? No. But you can do that! It requires discipline and repeated reminders to ourselves, but they are immensely rewarding!

Yes, they need to be reinforced again and again. And when you fail, are you disappointed? Very. But when you fail to live up to these, all is not lost. Failure is not always a disaster. You can learn from your failures. In fact failures can be what gets your serious attention and become one of life's important teachers. You can reprogram the mind and ask it to continue to guide you to give your best dreams their best chance to happen. You just must not give up. There are many tragic stories in our time that lead to the hall of shame. Yours need not be one of them. Your story can lead to the hall of fame!

When you are young, you have to juggle a lot of things at one time - assimilating new knowledge, adjusting to parental controls and thinking you are already mature enough to make your own decisions, even though the brain is not fully developed until you are twenty-five. You may have to put up with peers who make fun of you because you don't choose to do drugs, or sex, or drink alcohol. They may brag about how they are more courageous than you, when in fact, just the opposite is true. Some who venture into reckless behavior at so young an age are already programming their mind for big disappointments and will end up with sexually transmitted disease, pregnant, or the one who caused a pregnancy, or with addiction to drugs and alcohol, or with a criminal record, all resulting in a critical interruption of education and career goals. It's a recipe for failure, not success. Who, then, can be smart or wise? You!

So what, if people make fun of your devotion to a more wholesome life, let them look on down the road of life and see how your plan works and brings honor, while their lack of qualities lead to failed money management, lack of confidence, emotional weakness, social brokenness, and inner failure. It's like Solomon said, "*I would have you learn this great fact: that a life of doing right is the wisest life there is.*" *Proverbs 4:11*

Having made wise choices, you can look back and say, 'That's my story. That's what I did when I was young, when times were tough, and I made the hard choices which, in the long run, gave my story integrity in spite of being ridiculed. Now I can look back and be proud of my story.'

Camp Tekoa is a place where young people get a chance to stand outside their developing story enough to look at it and the identity being programmed into their own self-image. At Camp Tekoa you can do that along with other young people who are ready to define who they are, not by the world around them, so much as by ideals within. It's a chance to get your identity right.

But you don't have to be at Camp Tekoa for that to happen. You can listen to your inner dialogue, your inner storyteller, your wise counselor, where your own developing Identity Guidance System, your GPS, can help you define your best story right where you are.

What young campers anywhere have, is an inner talisman, ready to be programmed by those qualities which define and guide a wholesome and honorable life. Other names can be given for this inner talisman - future guide, a personal counselor, an inner voice, your better self, identity guidance system, your GPS - an inner storyteller who tells about the gifts which are ready for you to choose for your place in the story at a high level of honor and nobility. You may, or may not, be religious for this inner guide to work. You are creating your own story. It's up to you. Having the just right religion is not enough. You will need a faith in which you choose the Big Ten identity qualities, along with, or over and above religion.

For those who may have been campers at Camp Tekoa, or who are just imagining being at such a place, you can reflect on the closing campfire on the hillside across the lake. The closing campfire begins as a single camper comes up, bends down, and strikes a match to the pre-laid campfire. Flames begin slowly, then grow higher. Songs, one after another, become sounds of fun and laughter around the glow of the fire-lighted circle, surrounded by darkness beyond. Stories are told while the campfire flames die away into glowing embers. Great memories have now been written on the mind. The soft tones of Kum Bah Yah rise as, one by one, campers turn and walk away from the campfire circle, down the hill and across the dam of the lake. Darkness invades the pathway and stars appear in the night sky. Friendships have grown. A few boys and girls may even be holding hands in new bonds of friendship.

Many young people like yourselves, have observed a famous pianist, or violinist, or watched a great tennis player, or listened to a great speaker, and said, either verbally, or just in their own minds, *'That's what I want to be when I grow up.'* Later those dreams may become a part of their career. But even more important than seeing one's dream career is to see one's dream story as the story of a person who chooses to live out the Big Ten Universal Qualities at a level of excellence. So, go ahead. Dream your best dream. Dream a dream that, not only expects the best for you, but demands the best from you. Keep on giving your best dreams their best chance to happen!

On his first assignment, a young preacher went to visit a farmer. The farmer was drilling wheat with a forty thousand dollar drill, pulled by a big eighty thousand dollar tractor. The farmer saw the young preacher as he came walking across the field. He stopped his big tractor and climbed down to meet the young pastor. After greetings and handshakes, the young minister said, "I know you are busy and I don't want to take much time away from your important work, but I just wanted to say hello, and to ask your help. I hope you can help me know what to tell young people as I begin to serve here."

The farmer backed up a couple steps and leaned against the wheel of his big tractor. He said, 'I have all the time there is. There is no hurry. But, what I would say is, tell the young people to dream their best dream, and to ask successful older people about the wisdom they have gathered along the way.'

When you asked me to have a session just for young people, you let me be that man standing by his tractor, telling about wisdom, gathered along the way. What a privilege you gave me. Thank you!

CHAPTER NINE

For Such A Time As This
A New Day For
Religious Leadership

Every worship service should be a clinic
where we update our identity and define ourselves
in terms of new opportunity to make tomorrow better than yesterday.

WHEN DR. RAY HART CAME TO THE SPEAKER'S LECTERN, HE BEGAN by saying, "When we got here this evening there was a sign on the door - YOUTH SESSION IN PROGRESS. ADULTS PLEASE WAIT. I was impressed when I learned that our young people had asked Dr. Kelly to give a session just for them. He was immensely pleased with their request, so together, they had decided they could meet before this evening session. What a special privilege they had, and what a compliment to Dr. Kelly to give a session just for his new young friends. I have heard that he called them his newest grandchildren.

Now, I get to open the regular session and present Dr. Kelly, who has just shown what a special friend he is to young people.

However, the extra chairs, brought in for this event, make it evident that our guest speaker is a special friend to all of us and needs no introduction at all, just a chance to begin. Nevertheless." When Dr. Hart paused ever so briefly, people began to laugh, knowing it was a one word jest. "Nevertheless, I surely would be wasting a mighty good opportunity to tell you what you already know, and that is, what a privilege we have to have our guest speaker with us this evening. But, since you already know that, I just won't tell you. But what I can't quite figure out is why Dewey Campbell, as the dean of this event, didn't introduce me as the one who gets to introduce the speaker. So, I guess I will just have to do it myself. My name is." When he paused again, everyone had already caught on to his jesting manner and laughed again. "Well, since you already seem to know that, I won't tell you that either. All jesting aside, what I do want to say, and what I hope our guest speaker already knows, is that he is a highly esteemed and welcomed guest here! And we want him back every time he can come." An enthusiastic applause began immediately as an affirmation of that welcome. "Right now, I think I know what you want. You want me to stop so Dr. Kelly can start. So, with great pleasure, I now present to you, Dr. James Kelly."

As Dr. Kelly stepped forward, the handshake the two of them exchanged showed immense mutual respect. Dr. Kelly turned immediately to the audience and said, "Good evening, my special friends, and I do mean special. Being here has added a new dimension to my understanding of what it means to write in a time when there is such a great need for churches just like yours, and for volunteer program directors like Dr. Ray Hart.

I have never had an introduction quite like that. But what it did, was to make me feel very welcome, and I deeply appreciate that. It's a part of the warmth and uplift I feel every time I come here.

What I can tell you about Ray Hart is something you already know too, but I get to tell you as an expression of my esteem for him. You are so fortunate to have this man on your staff. What makes him even more special is that he is on staff, but not on salary, or any other kind of compensation, except the return of joy he gets from helping you to have, what I think is, the greatest program ministry of any church I know.

When we had lunch together today, I asked him to tell me about his philosophy of program ministry. He immediately explained that he and Reverend Carvelle do ministry with people, rather than for them. In a brief summary of his response, he said, 'What I do here as program director is to network the skills and gifts people into ministries of kindness and caring. We share ideas, paintings, books, study and discussion, worship, and service. We seek to utilize the talent base here, along with bringing in outstanding talent. While other churches are bringing in old fashion revival preachers, we are bringing in outstanding leaders and speakers who can update and expand our knowledge base so we can make informed and wise choices about how to live a great quality life in a brand new age.'

Dr. Hart kept going. He said, 'This in no way takes away from what happens in the sanctuary. Instead, it elevates it as we come together in reverence and respect for the wonders of all molecular existence. When we sing, pray, listen, and dream together, it is therapy and an identity update which we apply to our own varied journey stories. It's never trying to defend a theology or protect an institution, rather it's our way of making our faith into a living faith, flexible, open-ended, interfaced with our careers and service that heals hurts and expands dreams. We bring outstanding speakers to the conference center to update and advance our knowledge base so we can use it as information capital to invest in a wiser and more sustainable paradigm for our best story and a better future.

In no way does this displace the need for the Sunday School. Children are deprived for the rest of their life if they do not know the great stories of the Bible which are taught in Sunday School. The stories they learn become foundational metaphors

and a backdrop on paradigms that are important to know. Because
of what we do in both the conference center and sanctuary, our
children and youth know first hand that our worship, study, and
service are inextricable linked together.'

Dr. Hart was enthusiastic when he kept explaining his program
philosophy and said, almost like a challenge in a sermon, 'Why not
build a church program that defines who we are by the best dream
we can dream for our personal story and our quest for a great humanity? Why not live by a dream in which we build our best agriculture, our best home and family, our best career, our best health,
our best business, our best schools and education, our best church
and community, all of which can show our highest respect for the
sacred nature of all existence?' I liked his closing summation. He
said, 'Let that be the main business of the church!'

So, I know I am repeating to say this, but no wonder I feel such
an uplift when I come here. Every church needs somebody like
Ray Hart to help it be a faith in action, not theology to defend or
an institution to preserve.

We all need people around us whom we respect, and who
cause us to stand taller, and reach higher for the better side of our
humanity. Just talking with such a person, even on the phone,
can have this kind of reaching-up effect. We all need to have association with parents, grandparents, family members, neighbors,
teachers, fellow students, fellow workers, ministers, and friends
who help us lift our level of self esteem. We need books, sermons,
and daily associations which create that updraft of aspiration and
motivation to keep us trying to be those better persons that we
have the potential to be.

The great need is for a church to have integrity in the molecular age - to make sure that the underlying theme its people hear
at its centers of worship, learning, and activity, form an identity
framework in which the people say, 'I am a part of a world citizen
church! I am a world citizen!'

I am honored to be invited out here where you may be as

close to being a world citizen church as any other church I have known. I have to be on my best behavior just to justify my talking to people like you. Ever since that morning I stopped by for your Kindness Breakfast Bazaar five years ago, I have felt the surge of energy you are releasing here. And I want my book to reflect that understanding of a higher identity. So, thank you, for being a part of this writing process where you are giving me an audience that challenges me to write up to such positive expectations.

Let me ask, 'Which is better, to live on the holding edge of the past, or the leading edge of the future?' It's the same age, of course, except very different. It results in contrasting identity.

Which is better, to live on the authority-based side of the great divide, anchored in the past, or to cross over to the knowledge-based side, as an open-ended explorer of the future?

A walk through the National Air and Space Museum, near Dulles International Airport, lets us admire many of the creations which led former explorers to push forward on their new frontiers. New generations of boys and girls can look up at the sleek Concorde that once shuttled between the US and France, or look at the space shuttle "Enterprise," that has been retired after its journeys into space, and build dreams as they look. They may be observing the past, but they can be dreaming about the leading edge of their own future. Defining that future is what the new sacred is about.

Even as we walk around in the National Air and Space Museum, and marvel at the advances in engineering, we must remember that the qualities we live by are far more important than the products we create. There are no museums for the heroes of the Big Ten qualities, but there are treasured stories about new dreams for new tomorrows. Not everyone can work in a science research lab, or even wants to. Some had rather work on a farm, or in a home, or office, or school, or business. But wherever we live and work, we can live out the Big Ten Universal Qualities as our place in the story.

The goal is not for the Big Ten Universal Qualities ever to become the basis of a new religion. That would be a new mistake and freeze vision and promise. That's the mistake early Christians made of Jesus, and the mistake fundamentalists still make of him. They made Jesus into a religion, instead of letting him be the great philosopher and teacher of his time. Before that, it was the mistake Jewish religion made of the ideas of Moses. They made his movement into a religion, and then into a rigid legal code and system. Instead of freezing faith into a religion, the new sacred is open-ended, with the potential to synthesize knowledge, science, technology and our best qualities into new insights and the stories we live out.

It is my hope that a new generation of theology students will boldly 'go where no man has ever gone,' by boldly reaching across the great divide for a new paradigm of intellectual integrity which leads beyond theology to vision - to a working knowledge-based faith. It will take prophetic courage for a new generation of students to break free from theological bondage to the past, so they can be free to explore the future.

Breaking free is made even more difficult when well-known theologians and spokespersons come to the campus to speak, and are praised, celebrated, and given honorary doctoral degrees as great scholars, when, in fact, they are doing little more than warming over the old sacred, authority-based, transcendence paradigms. But escape velocity is possible. The world awaits its new prophets of courage to boldly lead the way where few have dared to go.

As a story base for all this, I want to tell the story of Esther, and her unique time of challenge and opportunity in one defining moment.

Esther faced a challenge like never before. It had to do with racism at its worst - with genocide. It brought her face to face with what she really believed in, whether it was only in herself, or something bigger and more important than her own safety. Her uncle, Mordecai, was the one who identified the critical nature of the challenge she faced.

The story begins with King Ahasuerus, emperor of Persia, throwing a big political party. I mean, a big party! Talk about knowing how to throw a party, he knew how to throw a party. It was for all the governors of his expansive empire that reached all the way from what is now Pakistan and Afghanistan, on up to Turkey, thence east to include most of the Black Sea coastal regions, and the territories of Iraq, Saudi Arabia, Jordan, Israel, Lebanon, Syria, and portions of Egypt and Libya. King Ahasuerus invited representatives from the entire region to come to his palace garden for a big party, with lots of food and all the wine anyone wanted to drink.

Eventually, King Ahasuerus did his part in the drinking. When he became so intoxicated that he became elated with his sense of power and importance, he invited his queen, Vashti, to come to the party and show off her beauty for the men. Well, guess what? She refused to do that! Really? Nobody does that! Or do they? Queen Vashti did. She refused to present herself in that sensual, subservient way. What an immediate embarrassment for the king and threat to his power. He was furious. What was worse, governors had come in from all across the empire to celebrate his power and prestige and now, his own queen refuses to obey his call! It was not only a threat to his manly powers, it could undermine the powers his governors held. King Ahasuerus saw it as a serious confrontation. It was pure defiance. It was insurrection, just as he was building his political influence. He just couldn't have that, right there in his own palace, could he? That story would spread like wild fire, and soon women from all those territories would disobey their husbands. It was a political nightmare. Queen Vashti's defiance would become revolutionary. And now, in our time, we just thought politics and public image were new, and that Gloria Steinem led the women's movement. What could the king do? He sought counsel among his key people. Their advice? Banish her. Get a new queen. Show political strength and do damage control. So, the king sent out a letter across the empire, that all women must be subject to their husbands. How do you think that went over?

But how can King Ahasuerus get a new queen? Answer. Have a beauty contest.

As word about the contest spread, Mordecai, a Jewish exile from Jerusalem, heard about it. That's when he thought about his niece, Esther, whom he had adopted after her parents died. He wanted her to enter the contest. So, Esther was one of many girls who entered the beauty contest. All the girls were sent to "charm school" and provided with a special diet to enhance their beauty. Then, one by one, each of them would spend time with the king. When Esther came to visit King Ahasuerus, he liked her so much that he set the royal crown on her head and she became his new queen.

All was going well until one day Uncle Mordecai refused to bow to the king's prime minister, Haman, who considered himself like a god. Insulted by this disloyalty, Haman set out to kill Mordecai. He even built a scaffold on which to hang him as an example of those who dared to defy his orders. In the process, he found out that Mordecai was Jewish, so then he upped his plot to kill, not only Mordecai, but all the Jewish people. He got authorization from King Ahaseurus, then rolled a dice to decide on which day to do it.

When Mordecai heard about this he was greatly distressed. Was there anyone who could intervene and stop this genocide? If anyone could, it would be Esther. She was the queen. She could enter a plea on their behalf. But if she did that, the king would find out that she was Jewish, and that she had shielded that information earlier by changing her name from the Jewish name, Haddassah, to Esther. Identifying herself as Jewish would mean she would not escape, even though she was the queen. She would be killed along with all the other Jewish people. To intervene on behalf of her people was a big, big risk. But her uncle knew that if she wanted to save her people, she had to take that risk. It was a defining moment. That's when he made that famous challenge.

> *"Do you think you will escape there in the palace, when all other Jews are killed? If you keep quiet at a time like this, God will deliver the Jews from some other source, but you and your relatives will die: what's more, who can say but that God has brought you into the palace for just such a time as this?'* (Esther 4:13-14)

Esther rose to the occasion and made an appearance before the king, at the risk of her life. As a result, her people were spared. Then the story took a new turn. Haman, the prime minister, who had built a scaffold on which he was going kill Mordecai, was hanged on that same scaffold and Mordecai was made the new prime minister. And you wonder where Shakespeare got some of his plots? But if you know Jewish traditions, you already know that this story is the inspiration behind the Jewish celebration of Purim, celebrated each year in Jewish synagogues.

Yes, it is a Jewish story, but it is more than that. It is a defining moment story, about how one person can shape the future. Esther took risks and used the position she held as a tool to save her people.

Fast forward across time and Queen Esther's defining moment of "for such a time as this," raises some very important questions about our, "for such a time as this."

One question which occurs is, **"What time is it, then, for the world family?"**

With the tools in our hands at this point in civilization's story? Isn't this the strategic time to link the capital resources of accumulative knowledge, global economies, the philanthropy of foundations, communication networks, collaboration forums, educational

enterprises, science and technology, information and communication - isn't our 'such a time as this, the time to build massive common cause on behalf of a better world and better people? If this is
humanism, let us make the most of it. If it is religion in transition
from being just a religion, over to being an overarching faith, let
us make the most of this opportunity to live on the leading edge
of the future instead of the holding edge of the past!

We have a chance to become the greatest generation! If the
Big Ten identity becomes the basis of personal choice for billions
of people in the world family, we will have fewer conflicts across
national borders and among clashing ideologies. We will have
fewer broken homes, and a decreasing number of people in prison.
We will have fewer violent conflicts which end in personal failures
and social tragedies.

But also, the question arises, "What time is it for the church
and its leadership for a positive, creative faith?"

We are entering a time when a partnership of science and technology with an overarching faith can advance us to new levels of
a higher and more noble humanity. This new identity will leave
behind the insistence on having the right theology, and reach ahead
for a vision theology which crosses all boundaries.

It is time to make our worship experiences into positive identity updates, where people come to adjust their self image, concur-
rent with modern knowledge about how the world works and how
we can work with the way it works to write a better future story.

There are many people who experience so much anger, hate,
hostile feelings, bitterness, and lack of trust, that it gets acted out
in violence and self destruction across all human societies. People
need study and worship experiences which give them ways to find
release from inner turmoil and conflict. All of us need a faith that
breathes new life and hope into who we see ourselves as being.
Every worship service should be an experience in healing the
mind and feelings. It should be a time to measure by the uplift

of the big dreams set by the Big Ten Universal Qualities - a time to reshape paradigms so we can reshape our story and our future! Worship should be a therapy event where people respect each other's struggles which are a part of life in an imperfect world, and who, in turn, share friendship and caring to help each other turn old endings into new beginnings as new winners.

So, I have great hope and expectations for the church. I am very much pro-church. I want to see thousands of churches become centers for teaching and learning the Big Ten as an identity umbrella under which we build networks of trust and celebrate the call of a more noble humanity.

But, in this new world of great possibilities, what happens for many people at the church they choose to attend, is that their identity is handicapped - defined by a reinforcement of the old sacred. They sing songs which define life's struggles as, not their fault or responsibility, because some bright morning they will "fly away" to the great escape in the sky and leave all their troubles behind. Some repeat the Apostles Creed which defines a sweeping worldview of history from beginning to end, as God's rescue plan for life after death, instead of defining their opportunity to live a great life here and now. They hear sermons based in doctrines to be believed, instead of dreams to be explored. They share discussions in classes, and among networks of friends who are more likely to find fault with things as they are, rather than working to make things become what they ought to be. In short, they reinforce negative stories about themselves and their world. It becomes a dominating sunset paradigm. Whatever they have encountered in the past week, it's not their fault. The cause is from some demonic force, over which they have no control - "The devil made me do it," as comedian Flip Wilson used to say. The standard assumption is that only some miracle from outside can help. So, they get a sense of emotional escape and momentary high, as they sing, "How Great Thou Art," and reinforce old views of how God is going to take care of everything, "When

Christ shall come with shout of acclamation and take me home, what joy shall fill my heart."

But in churches where the new sacred is the overarching sunrise paradigm, they hear a positive view of life in which people find recurring encouragement to choose a new and better future – that, in spite of yesterday's failures, and today's struggles, tomorrow is a new day, with new possibilities and accountability. Instead of trying to undo yesterday, they hear about working to create a new tomorrow. They hear about being more pleasant persons, more diplomatic, with better health, more fulfillment, joy, purpose, meaning, and a more successful life. It is an identity update, shaped by a better dream. The quest is to be better people who, in turn, make a better world. The promise of the future builds as millions adopt the guiding, uplifting, markers of the Big Ten Universal Qualities.

So, in a quest to make better dreams come true, these persons of an overarching faith sing:

> This is a day of new beginnings,
> Time to remember and move on,
> Time to believe what love is bringing,
> Laying to rest the pain that's gone.[14]

Every worship experience should be an identity update. Every worship leader should be an identity therapist. Worship leaders can use the word tools of the Big Ten to define, redirect, and channel the best healing emotions. Services at places of worship can be an experience in motivation to use our talents and build career skills to enrich life for ourselves and others. Worship can inspire us to add to our knowledge base and build our skills for new levels of service. Stories from yesterday can be told as metaphors that inspire a reach for new tomorrows. Whether we meditate, pray, sing, or listen to

---

[14]   Brian Wren

messages, we can be challenged to do the best of things in the worst of times as a succession of new beginnings beyond old endings.

Worship can be a valuable time of healing. What often gets any of us into difficulty, in our own life story, is the negative self-images we nurture, the grudges, bitterness, disappointment, anger, and hostility we harbor inside. Worship can be an experience which defuses anger by building feelings of confidence that we can transcend the brokenness of yesterday in a persistent reach for new tomorrows. That's worship at its best."

When Dr. Kelly paused a moment from his excited monologue, one lady raised her hand and quietly entered a question, with a personal preface. "Dr. Kelly, my name is Betsy. I have three children, young adults now. They grew up in the church, but as for their interest in the church, it has dropped off the radar. They aren't hostile toward the church, they just don't see it as relevant - don't seem to be on the same wave length any more. That doesn't mean they aren't good people. They are. The best. And if you think this is just another mother bragging about her children, maybe it is, but it's also because they really are the best of people. But as I listen to you, I keep wishing they could be here to hear what you are saying. I wish they could be in a church like this. I get the feeling they are a part of the new sacred, but have never had anyone to help them define it as an open-ended faith. Could that be the case?"

"Betsy," Dr Kelly answered kindly, "That is the case for many people in our time, young or old. So, I'm not sure which dropped off the radar first, your children, or the church, or religion in general. I just know the world has changed, while the church has not changed along with it enough to be the voice of the future, 'crying in the wilderness' as a new John the Baptist.

Your question is so right for this moment. It has to do with updating our faith. Let me refer to the way Jesus, in his time, called for an update of one's faith. He said that, when an ox falls in a ditch, get it out. It doesn't matter that it's the Sabbath, and against the rules of religion, it's time to get busy and get the ox out of the ditch. Whenever the proverbial ox is in the ditch, new criteria comes into play. When the knowledge base changes, as it has in the molecular age, new guiding markers apply that overarch the old rules so that a greater good displaces a lesser good as a new and higher right.

The ox is in the ditch for the church. The times call for immanence, but many people are still responding with a transcendence paradigm. The trust level is running low because in so many churches, their paradigms are frozen in time, and in literal interpretations of ancient sacred texts. It's not a faith, it's a religion. It is protected by a wall of fear and guilt, and honored by subservience to tradition and rigid systematic theology.

In contrast, worship can be a way to find release from that kind of bondage to the past. Hence, every worship service should be a clinic where we update our identity and define ourselves in terms of new opportunity to make tomorrow better than yesterday. That's worship that helps us enter our best request of life for such a time as this!

Wow. I get wound up, don't I? Even so, I realize that it's not only break time, it's beyond break time. Let's take a break and have some refreshments, so generously provided by our friends.

CHAPTER TEN

Profile Of A Hero

Our greatest heroes will be
those who honor humanity at its best
and serve humanity's most noble causes.

WHEN DR. KELLY BEGAN THE SECOND SECTION, HE WAS ALMOST apologetic. He said, "That last session was too long, but I had so much I wanted to say about the identity and mission of the church, that I may have gotten a bit carried away. So, all the more thanks to those who provided the re-energizing refreshments at the break. As usual, all the variety of good things to eat on that elaborate table were super delicious. Thanks so much!

Let me begin by responding to a question Varlena Harrell asked me during break. She's one of your college students, and you would be proud of the question she asked. I didn't have time to respond fully then and asked her if I could take it up in the next session. Varlena asked me how I saw science and technology and a knowledge-based faith coming together in a partnership. What I said to her then was that we need the help of many inquiring, learned, informed, and wise persons to imagine and explore an answer. It's such an extensive question, but let me give it a condensed answer.

I think we know that most of the answer has to do with resetting human behavior to align with the qualities of the Big Ten, and at the same time respecting our growing knowledge base in science.

Part of the answer may be in the arena of neuroscience, where the identity we choose can shape our brain so that it will guide us to less conflicting images and behaviors. Part of the answer is in the arena of genetic engineering with increasing potential to make corrections in genetic information. Part of the answer needs to come from the arena of nano-technology, where nano corrections are made to out-of-control cells. In our new crossovers among the sciences, where we are dealing with intricate and complex processes, we realize that we need to discover all the ways we can to become better persons. Our exploration question becomes, 'What will make us better?' One answer is to celebrate our best heroes.

The greatest heroes of the future will be those who align science and technology with the highest qualities of humanity, blended together in their own stories that model the wholesome qualities of the Big Ten. It matters not whether the heroes in our stories live in a mansion or cottage, have wealth or live with limited finances, or whether they are formally educated or learned in the varied avenues of experience - what matters is that when they respect and honor the best of humanity's highest qualities, they qualify as heroes.

These heroes may, or may not, command high visibility, just high respect. The school teacher who is seeking to end illiteracy is a hero. Parents who guide children and youth to have character and discipline are heroes. Career persons who choose to make their careers their stage for honorable service will be among our greatest heroes. The stage doesn't matter as much as the quality of life played out on the stage, where we respect all that science can teach us and all that the Big Ten can do to guide our identity and choices.

Life's big questions are sometimes answered in stories. Our best stories are about how heroes can help us see ourselves and what is important in our own story. So, let me tell you a story out of real life as a profile of a hero.

The phone rang in Ben Daniel's office suite, on the fourteenth floor of the Clark Tower in downtown Wacoma. Ben was usually the first to arrive, so his administrative assistant was not there yet, when the phone rang. Ben picked up the phone, and in his pleasant and cordial manner said, "Good morning. This is Ben Daniel. How can I be helpful?"

"Good morning, Mr. Daniel," the caller said. "This is Karen Holmes with the Wacoma Times. I am doing a series of stories on successful business leaders and I am calling to see if you would be willing to tell me your story of how you have come to be one of Wacoma's well-known, and highly regarded leaders. May I come to your office at your convenience and listen to your story?"

"I would be pleased to share my story," Ben said. "It's really very simple, but if you think it can be helpful, I will be glad to share it."

When Karen arrived later that morning she was graciously received by the receptionist at the main entrance, and then after that, by Mr. Daniel's administrative assistant, Maria Karina.

"Mr. Daniel is expecting you," Maria said, as she stood, then led the way to Mr. Daniel's office.

"Hello Karen," Ben said, as he stood immediately and walked around his desk, with his hand extended in a cordial welcome. "I'm pleased to see you," he said cordially. "You honor me by your request. Let's sit over here on the side where we can relax. 'Maria, would you like to bring us some coffee and pastries?'"

As soon as they were seated, Ben said, "Karen, how does a

young reporter get an assignment like this? You must have done well in your profession. And do you have a family? I would like to know your story?"

It wasn't what Karen had expected as a way to begin. It was an extension of Ben's sincere interest in many people, which Karen had already heard about, but was now seeing in person. After sharing a brief summary, Karen said, "And now, Mr. Daniel, can you tell me how you became a successful leader?"

"How far back do you want me to go?" Ben asked. "And, you don't need to call me, Mr. Daniel. Just call me, Ben. It's short for Benjamin, but nobody ever calls me that. I am known as Ben."

"Well, as far back as you can, or want to go," Karen replied.

"How about if I begin with when I was twelve years old," Ben said. "That's when my career story really begins. My granddad was a successful businessman in our small town. One day I said, 'Granddad, you've made a success of your business here, and I want to be a businessman when I grow up. Can you tell me the secret of your success?'

Granddad chose his words slowly as he said, 'You make me very proud to hear you say that.' Then he picked up the pace and enthusiasm in his words and said, 'But I can do better than that. I can show you how to start your own business.'

'But, Granddad, I'm only twelve years old,' I deflected, astonished at his offer.

'Twelve years old is an excellent age for starting a business, Ben, if you are really serious about it.'

'I'm serious,' I said. 'Tell me all you know.'

That's when he said, with a warm sense of guidance in his voice, 'First of all, we already know what your business will be. It will be one of honest and sincere service. Oh, it may rotate around one, or a thousands products, but your business will be service. Your business will begin with a search for a service that is needed somewhere, with you being the one who can fill that needed service. So, can you tell me something that is needed?'

I thought a moment and said, 'Well, Mr. Long's lawn needs mowing.'

'Okay,' he said, 'What is the name of a business you could start to fill that need? Let me help you a little. Whatever you call it, remember that it will be a service.'"

Ben paused and looked across his office and into the distance, as though he were looking back on that moment from yesterday, then turned a little more toward Karen. "Granddad asked me if I could invest ten dollars to start a business. Proudly, I said that I could, and that I had even more than that. He pursed his lips a little and moved his head up and down slightly. 'Ten dollars will be enough,' he said.

So with that, we began. I say "we" because he was my mentor. We went down the street to Ted's New and Used Lawn Mowers, and he told Ted that I wanted to go into business and needed a really good used mower, and that I could pay only five dollars for it.

I couldn't believe what I was hearing. I was embarrassed to offer so little. But while Ted went to look over his inventory of old mowers, Granddad told me about a business principle he followed. He said, 'Invest wisely with only what you can afford. You have ten dollars to start your business. You need to have some capital left for gas and oil and some for advertising.' We followed Ted and he showed us a push mower we could have for five dollars. Granddad told me to look it over, shake the wheels and look at the wear on the tires to determine how much it had been used.

We purchased that mower and I proudly pushed that old green lawn mower down the street. We cleaned it up, changed the oil, put in a new spark plug and got it running. It was fine.

That's when Granddad talked to me about advertising my new business. He said, 'We have to get the word out some way that you have a service to provide.' He helped me figure how much it would cost to make some copies of a flyer on a copier. Then he projected that we could buy some zip-lock bags and put a flyer into each bag, along with a little rock, and then pitch them out in people's driveways. When I suggested with excitement that he could drive me down the street and let me pitch them out, he said, 'Oh, no. I would have to charge you so much per mile and that would use up some more of what little money you have left after buying the oil, gas, making copies, and purchasing zip lock bags. I would be glad to do it for you, but you are going into business and you will need to keep a ledger account of everything you invest so you can know if your business is profitable.' So, I walked up one side of the street and then down the other side, pitching out those flyers in each driveway.

Then Granddad had me to make a sign on the back side of an old poster board, that I could hold up as I walked back and forth in front of my house. In big, bold letters it said, BEN'S LAWN MOWING SERVICE. Below that, in bold numbers, I put my phone number. That's all it said. He told me that's what I had to offer - service, and that I was now ready to deliver that service - that I was in business.

It worked. Soon the phone was ringing and I was mowing lawns, and getting paid for it. It was exciting. But he warned me to keep the focus on service. He said, 'Give the best service you can render and don't worry about the income. If you will prove yourself worthy of it, the income will come. Make sure you render great service.'

So, Karen, that's the story of whatever success I have achieved. Since that twelve- year-old beginning, I have ventured into other businesses, all of which are some kind of extension of that first enterprise."

Maria brought in the refreshments. As they shared them to-gether, Karen said, "Your granddad must have been a very special person. Can you tell me more about him?"

"My granddad's name was Solomon. They called him Sol. What I know about business I learned from him, and that little beginning. Now people come into my office suite here in the Clark Tower and think this office defines who I am. But who I am is not defined by this office, or where I live in town, so much as by what Granddad taught me.

Granddad said, 'Service is your business. Always give more and better service than you get paid for. Exceed expectations. The pay will come, but your service is part of your identity - your credibility. It has to do with your integrity, your honor, your character, who you are.' Yes, he used those big words. He said, 'It defines you as one who gives, instead of one who is out to get. Let what you plan to give to life always be your request of life. Don't worry, if you give, you will get. Your service will build respect and trust.'

Then Granddad added, 'Learn people's names. It's part of the kindness and congeniality you offer as part of your service. It shows that you value them as persons and not just for their business dealings. And, don't ever forget to be kind. That must not be just an add-on. It must be a part of who you are. It is part of being a giving person.'"

Ben paused to take a bit of pastry and sip of coffee, then continued eagerly. "There were other things I learned from my granddad. He said, 'To increase your service you will need to do three things. First, increase your knowledge base. Go to the library. Search on the internet. Go to college. And, learn from experience. Learn all you can, all your life. Second, never be afraid to collaborate with others who know more than you. Expand your knowledge base through others to expand your service. Collaborate. Network. There will always be people who know more than you. You need their help. You won't ever stop needing their help. So, network with others. There must be no boundaries to knowledge and co-operation with others to expand your service. Third, be kind to everyone. Nobody will ever forget it.'

"My granddad's philosophy about cooperation and kindness let me learn more than just how to start a business. It let me learn who he was, and who I wanted to be.

Now, Karen, I could go on and on, but that's what I credit for my success, what I learned from Granddad Solomon, beginning at twelve, with that old push mower.

I don't know how much time you have, but could I add in a little story?"

"Take as much time as you like," Karen said quickly.

"Grandparents are important heroes and heroines. Let me tell you what I saw the other day. I saw a living picture of the legacy grandparents can generate, ever so quietly. I had gone on an overnight excursion into the mountains along the Blue Ridge Parkway. My wife was attending a convention in Denver, Colorado. So I took an overnight and next day excursion of my own. At lunch time that next day, I turned off the Parkway into Julian Price Park for a picnic snack lunch. It was crowded and there were no picnic tables available. I circled a while and finally pulled in at an empty parking space. This would have to be my picnic spot. I opened the skylight, then touched the window buttons to roll down all four windows. I got out my little snack lunch and began to have my picnic.

In front of me, under the trees and along the edge of a small mountain stream, another picnic was beginning. A long picnic table was laden with food, including buckets of Colonel Sander's fried chicken. Down on one side of an elongated circle, younger members of the family were seated in lawn chairs, or just standing around, or tossing things back and forth in playful and restless activity. One college age couple was obviously sharing in the touches of young romance as the young man put his arms around his girlfriend and leaned around and kissed her. Soon the younger members of this extended family began to stand in a kind of beginning circle. They began to reach out and join hands. On around the encircled table, others got up from their lawn chairs and joined the circle. Up at the end of the circle, grandmother slowly got up from her chair and became a part of the family circle. Granddad stepped into the circle and reached out to take her hand, then reached out for the hand of another person to complete the circle. The young men took off their caps and bowed their heads. Then granddad began a prayer. I couldn't hear his words, but I noted that it lasted a full minute. Then, caps went back on and the picnic was instantly in full surge. It was a moment in which respect and esteem were a part of a silent drama.

Grandparents are living metaphors of a longer view of the journey of life. They represent an extended stewardship of a place in the story. When they have lived that story with honor, they are held in high esteem as persons who model something worthy of respect, something sacred. When, as sometimes happens, a new baby has been born, and that new baby is tenderly placed in the arms of a grandparent, an artist could paint that picture and entitle it, 'the promise of the future'.

Now, Karen, I have stopped telling you my story you asked for, and have been sharing my philosophy of life. Of course, it's in our stories that we often capture the essence of life and bring life's passages into living pictures which show who we are."

A moment of thoughtful silence followed before Karen said, "Ben, I can't help but think your philosophy is part of the story I want most to tell. But, now, please tell me something else. Tell me that you still have that old lawn mower."

"I do, in fact," Ben said enthusiastically, " and I am glad I kept it. It's kind of a symbol for me."

"Could I come to your house at your convenience and take a picture of it?" Karen asked.

"I will be very pleased for you to take a picture of it," Ben said with obvious pride. "But you won't need to come to my house to find it. It's right here in my office, behind the door of a special little glass room, or should I say, shrine. Strange as it may seem to some people, I built a little room for it right here in my office. And right beside the door are two framed quotations I saved from my granddad's office, after he died. Together these framed quotations form a little capsule of whatever success I have been privileged to put together."

Steve pointed to the framed quotations on the wall, and said, "These are treasurers I have kept across the years. After Granddad died, I took them from his office wall and brought them to my office. And though I have changed offices a few times since that first office, these framed quotations have been on my office walls ever since. They help me to think in terms of the art of the possible. They help me to think hope in the face of challenge, and to know that there is little reward for easy victories.

One is a quotation from George Washington Carver, the world famous scientist who was an early predecessor of bioengineering, which is such an important part of modern agriculture. I remember Granddad telling Mr. Carver's story every time he got a chance. We can step closer to read the quotation. I never tire of reading it. Mr. Carver said, IT'S NOT THE STYLE OF CLOTHES ONE WEARS, NEITHER THE KIND OF AUTOMOBILE ONE DRIVES, NOT THE AMOUNT OF MONEY ONE HAS IN THE BANK, THAT COUNTS. THESE MEAN NOTHING. IT IS SIMPLY SERVICE THAT MEASURES SUCCESS.

Service is still the measure of success. Service is connecting ideas. It's about connecting information, digitally, or in person, or through products, it's all service. And so, Karen, you are engaged in service. A story connects. Readers want to see reflections of their own stories, mirrored in other people's stories. It's a service. And in our time, service is expanding exponentially through digital and scientific technology. The thing that makes life so exciting in our time is that we get to be a part of it. We have a place in the story.

Stories have heroes. Not only was my granddad my hero, George Washington Carver was his hero, not actually in person, but by way of knowing his story. In a nutshell, Mr. Carver was a person who worked in the realm of science, analogous to bio-mimicry long before there was such a science. He studied nature. He made new products from what nature has given. He made 300 different products from peanuts, 118 from sweet potatoes, and 75 from pecans. And he did all that starting from the bottom. I mean, from the very bottom. He was the son of slave parents. He was not a strong child so he stayed around the plantation house instead of working in the fields. Then he got a break - he was allowed to go to a nearby school. He stayed in school across the years until he earned a Masters Degree. He worked for a while at Iowa State University. One day he got an invitation from Booker T. Washington to come to the Tuskegee Normal and Industrial Institute, in Tuskegee, Alabama, which he had founded five years earlier. Mr. Carver accepted that invitation. He taught in that school and did his research there until he died, forty-seven years later, in 1943. During that time he became world famous as a scientist and met with three American presidents, Theodore Roosevelt, Calvin Coolidge, and Franklin D Roosevelt. He was once invited to tell about his work before a congressional committee. He was given ten minutes to speak, but that spellbound committee extended his time again and again, and then stood in enthusiastic applause when he finished.

He was a personal friend to Henry Ford and collaborated with him on soy beans as an alternative fuel. In 1942, Mr. Ford built a replica of Mr. Carver's slave cabin in the Henry Ford Museum in Dearborn, Michigan.

The George Washington Carver National Monument was established in 1951 on 210 acres of the Missouri farm on which he was born.

Just like Granddad, I like to tell the story because it shows that we don't have to have ideal situations in order to give something important to life - just the courage to begin with what we have and make something good out of it. George Washington Carver was not only Granddad's hero, he is one of the early heroes for lots of people. They begin to think that if he could make so much from so little, they could too, if they would live with enough daring to venture and take a bite out of Eve's apples, outside the garden of Eden. Now, I've gotten off onto another story and deep into another metaphor.

Here is the other framed document I saved from my granddad's office. It lists ten qualities Granddad said were basic for success for anyone, anywhere, anytime. I don't know where he got them, perhaps he put them together himself, but he measured himself by those ten defining qualities. Those are the qualities I keep trying to measure by. Like the Carver quote I just read, I like to read these ten words also. They always help me to reach up to a new level. As you can see from their stair step arrangement, four of them lead up to a little landing, and then on up to the next level. So, **kindness, caring, honesty,** and **respect** lead up to the next level of **collaboration, tolerance, fairness** and **integrity.** Then, two words indicate a summit, **Diplomacy** and **Nobility.** Those represent a word picture and story of what Granddad tried to live out. They have to do with identity. Believe me, it's always a challenge to live up to these framed identity markers, but I keep trying.

If those words are lived out in a marriage, they would keep marriages from getting into trouble. All too often, marriage partners make a hell out of what started out in heaven. It doesn't have to be that way. Any two people who will build these qualities into their marriage, will find themselves in a better marriage because they will be putting better quality into their lives and relationships. This is especially true when they run into tough spots, or when one partner suffers from major sickness. There are many opportunities in a marriage to let those words, spoken so easily on the wedding day, "for better for worse," mean something special, and show who we really are in life's defining situations all down across the years.

What percentage of the world's population is in a marriage? I don't know, but it's a major percentage. So, it is one of the most important places to build these ten defining qualities into relationships. It can best be done from the very beginning, but also later, after things begin to crumble and couples need to reach out and find these defining words for their own marriage partnership. Ten words. Talk about words which can define who we are, I think those are among the most needed.

Now, the one word which leads all the rest is kindness. Kindness between parents is all important. Next comes kindness between parents and their children. Do you have any idea how many parents think they own their children and think they have the right to boss them around, even abuse them, with unkind words and harsh actions? Some parents aren't even kind to their children and youth - treat them like things, not young persons. They may give them lots of things or money, but if they don't speak kindly and respectfully to them as real persons they miss one of life's golden opportunities. Parents should listen to their children with kindness. They should teach them to be kind to each other. When children don't experience respect through kindness, something goes wrong inside. They become hostile, bitter, angry, defiant, and rebellious. How many people, who are in prison now, do you think would not be there if only they had grown up where kindness was the modus operandi of daily life? I don't know the percentage, but I think it is high. And one might go on to wonder how many would gradually find healing inside their minds, build positive relationships, and learn how to make better choices, if they would make kindness their guiding identity marker each day, wherever they are, even in prison. Of course, that is measuring by extremes. But people in any walk of life, anywhere, will find better tomorrows simply by making kindness their entrée every day.

Now, Karen, please excuse. I've quit telling you my story and begun telling you my philosophy again. But that is part of my story too, because, you know where I got a lot of this philosophy? I got it from Granddad, who was rightly named after the king of wisdom, King Solomon. My granddad became a living proverb for me, and, I might add, for many others. He was my hero!

I don't expect you to be able to put all this in your article, but it's all part of my story."

Karen responded immediately, but thoughtfully. "But I will put it in my article. Not word for word, but it will be there as a part of your story.

And, now, Ben, would you like to pull out that old lawn mower from its little shrine, as you call it, and may I take a picture of it and your framed quotations, with you standing beside them, with your hands on the handle of the old lawn mower?"

Karen snapped pictures from different angles, and then spoke in a tone of voice that indicated that she had the story she wanted. As she reached out to shake hands with Steve, she held on a moment longer to show her respect. She said, "This will be a story I can write with pride and pleasure. Thank you, Ben. Or, may I say, as a tribute of grateful respect, Thank you, Mr. Daniel."

The collective progression of the highest qualities in our human story, and the great causes of our time, are redefining what it means to be a hero. Heroes, of any time, have defining moments when they incorporate the finest qualities of the human family into daily life, often with little or no fanfare, or even any real recognition. They become silent leaders and models. They simply honor what they believe to be of great importance, no praise needed.

One hero in our time is a man named Nicholas Negroponte. A few years ago he realized that if children in the impoverished places in the world only had a laptop computer they would have the world of knowledge at their fingertips. So he began a program of giving thousands of little green laptop computers to children. And, while others have now joined the cause in different ways, he remains the one who led the way. It's right to include him as a hero of the molecular age.

Some heroes are defined by acts of nobility carried out when they had no idea that those acts of caring were even being observed, much less being heroic. They were just moments of unselfish devotion. This is dramatically represented in the story behind a little painting that has become a statuette some people put in their libraries, called, "Praying Hands."

Two brothers in a poor family near Nuremberg faced a dilemma. They both wanted to be artists but knew their father could never afford to send both of them to Nuremberg to study at the Academy. They worked out a pact. One would work in the mines to support the other while he studied. Then they would switch roles.

They tossed a coin on a Sunday morning after church and Albrecht Durer won the toss and went off to study, and Albert went to work in the mines. Albrecht became successful in his art and was beginning to earn good fees. His return to the village was celebrated with a grand dinner where he made a toast and announced that his brother could now go study while he took care of him. But Albert stood and declined, showing his hands, marked by work in the mines, and now with so much arthritis that he couldn't even hold a paint brush. Sometime later his brother sketched those weathered hands stretched skyward, as a tribute of honor to the sacrifices his brother had made for the opportunity he had to paint. Sculptured as bookends, or as paintings framed on our home or office walls, we look at those "Praying Hands" with respect and remind ourselves of the qualities that define our finest heroes.

It is most likely that all of you know stories of persons whose gifts to life made them heroes in your story. Norman Vincent Peale was one of those for me. I heard him speak only once, but I met him through his books. He dared to put faith above theology as he presented his messages about the power of positive thinking. Some fellow ministers criticized him, but many more were grateful that he kept on believing in possibilities which are the product of positive thinking.

Napoleon Hill was one of my heroes. He gleaned a central and leading concept from a mix of ideas that the way we think is what leads to a successful life-story. *Think and Grow Rich,* was more than the title of his well-known book, it taught people how to discipline their thoughts so they could believe in themselves and possibilities.

Without knowing who said it, I was told early in my life that all I needed was a few good books. Now I realize that one of those good books is the book of *Proverbs*. At the same time I was reading Solomon's proverbs as a boy, Jesus of Nazareth became my boyhood hero. He didn't need to be thought of as a God in order for me, and millions of others, to believe in his mustard seed faith. His "second-mile" philosophy of life, and his "give and gifts will be given to you" principle of recycled positive energy, are sunrise paradigms which expand the art of the possible. In that sense he lives on for the millions who dare to see him as the builder of an open-ended faith in the kingdom of unfinished dreams.

CHAPTER ELEVEN

The Big Ten
Smart Church

*A place in the story - that's all any of us ever
get, but that is no small place!*

DREW CARVELLE STOOD AT THE PULPIT ON SUNDAY MORNING AND
paused a moment to give his words added emphasis. When he began he said, "As minister at Center Church, I can speak for all of us
in saying that having Dr. James Kelly with us this week has been a
highlight event. We are all deeply grateful for his insights into the
new sacred. So, to you, Dr. Kelly, I speak for all of us in saying,
'Thank you, so much for what you have done for all of us here.'"

Turning back to the audience, Reverend Carvelle said, "As a
pleasant surprise, what has come together as part of this event is
the way Janet Miller and Tim Minton have done some collaboration of their talents and have put the words of Dr. Kelly's Big
Ten Universal Qualities into a song. So, Tim is going to lead us in
singing that song after Janet introduces it."

Janet walked out to the center of the chancel and looked out
across the audience with excitement in her face. She said, "Tim

and I have had a lot of fun putting this song together. Maybe I should say, 'crafting' it together, because we simply took some of Dr. Kelly's words and shaped them into a song. We've laughed at ourselves for trying such a bold idea, because neither of us can make any claims to poetic fame, and we know it. And soon you will know it, too. But we went ahead anyway. It's just that we wanted some new way we could show our appreciation for the ten words Dr. Kelly has defined anew for us.

The song we have written borrows from the cadence and tune of Natalie Sleeth's *Hymn of Promise*. But our metaphors are not nearly up to hers. Her metaphors are beautiful. Listen.

> In the bulb there is a flower;
> in the seed, an apple tree;
> in cocoons, a hidden promise:
> butterflies will soon be free!
> In the cold and snow of winter
> there's a spring that waits to be,
> unrevealed until its season,
> something God alone can see.[15]

Although her song is in our hymnal, and we sing it from time to time, our organist will play it once so we can have the tune in mind. Then, using the tune for *Hymn of Promise*, we can sing our new song together as a way to reinforce Dr. Kelly's ideas about the new sacred. And it can be an expression of appreciation for Dr. Kelly's having shared the special words of the Big Ten with us. So, follow the words in the bulletin and let's sing together, as Tim leads us in, "The New Sacred."

> There's a kindness for every pathway,
> Honesty in all we say.

---

[15]   Natalie Sleeth. *Hymn of Promise*.

There's respect for every caring,
    Qualities that lead the way.
There is vision on new horizons,
    We can climb and look to see,
The new sacred ever nearer,
    Waiting now for you and me.

Collaboration is in our future,
    Tolerance and integrity.
Fairness leads tomorrow,
    Joining with diplomacy.
Nobility crowns our heroes,
    Honoring high qualities,
The new sacred ever nearer,
    Waiting now for you and me.

We can claim each new promise,
    As one we can make to be,
Turning each old ending,
    Into paths we begin anew.
There is hope in each tomorrow,
    We can claim for our today,
The new sacred ever nearer,
    Waiting now for you and me.

When Revered Carvelle returned to the pulpit, he said, "Now we know Dr. Kelly is not the only writer here. Janet and Tim have just let us know about two more. What a nice addition to this very special time we are sharing together on new pathways.

What I think is that the introduction Janet has just given, has made a unique presentation of our guest speaker today, to which I need add very little, except, to express again our immense gratitude to Dr. Kelly for being with us here this past week and sharing an inside view of his new book in progress, with the working title of

A Place In The Story. And we are eager to listen again to his insights. So I now present to you the distinguished writer and friend, who has become our mentor for exploring new tomorrows, Dr. James Kelly!"

When Dr. Kelly came to the pulpit, his beginning words were quietly simple, "I want to express a sincere thanks to all of you who have made my writing into a collaborative exploration. Yes, I know. I did most of the talking but you were great listeners. Your kindness has led the way in making this a delightful venture together. We all can express our thanks to Janet and Tim for the song they have written and introduced. It's a delightful way of saying in a few minutes what I have taken four evenings to try to say. Maybe I should try writing songs instead of books."

A reflective tone was in his voice as he said, "It is good to stand in the pulpit again. Since my retirement, I have devoted myself mostly to my writing, teaching, and various speaking events. What a high privilege all of you have given me to be here with you at Center Church and to share in your friendship ministry. It has been a renewal of confidence that the country boy in me has something to say that someone wants to hear. Any serious speaker is flattered by a respectful audience. You have been that audience. I am grateful that, your young, most cordial distinguished minister, and friend to all of us, Reverend Carvelle, has given me the opportunity to give the sermon in this service. So, let me talk about, 'Our Legacy, and Our Request of Life.'

Since a sermon is supposed to have a text, let me quote one. Or, two. How about three? Two are from Proverbs. *'The wise man looks ahead.'* Proverbs 14:8. Next, *'The intelligent man is always open to new ideas. In fact, he looks for them.'* Proverbs 18:15. The other is from Matthew's biography of Jesus. What Matthew said in his book about his special friend from Nazareth, is that faith is a working dynamic, that the future we ask for, becomes an energizing request of life. It is an ongoing process that begins to happen while we are asking. So, Jesus said, '*Ask, and you will be given what you ask for. Seek and you will find. Knock, and the door will be opened. For everyone who asks, receives. Anyone who seeks, finds. If only you will knock, the door will open.*' Matthew 7:7, 8. In the Greek text, it is in the present imperative tense, which indicates an ongoing process, and includes the important word, "while." So, while we are asking, while we are seeking, and while we are knocking, that's when we can expect the oneness of life forces will come together in new ways as a vital energizing force in our own story. It's the way life works. And, it's the way we can work with the way life works. So, what happens in the developing story will be our request of life, and become our legacy.

When I was a boy I read from the book of *Proverbs*. King Solomon's proverbs are little sayings, one after another, that direct the mind to think on the winning side of life. They are about new paradigms for wise living - about thinking ahead so you can make choices that result in life's best rewards and fewest pitfalls. As a result of following these proverbs, we can be smarter, happier, more successful, and enjoy a more wholesome life.

In my writing I try to update that wise approach as new identity markers for our age of molecular oneness. I want to help people reach for the best from life by giving the best to life. I believe that can happen as we input the Big Ten Universal Qualities into the brain as a template by which it, in turn, guides our winning story. It's a look-ahead mind set, or philosophy, or psychology, or common sense way of entering life's best signals into our identity, so we can self-program at the upper level of our potential. It is a reach for a rewarding common ground goal of building a better world by being better people. This umbrella of identity defines a winning legacy we can leave behind as our 'footprints on the sands of time.'

Remember those highway signs you see once in a while, such as, 'You just passed the best pizza place in town. Do not pass 'go.' Go back three blocks to TEDS FAMOUS PIZZA.'

Makes me think of a story about two over zealous preachers who were standing on the side of the road, waving white flags beside a big sign they had created. In bold letters the sign said, "STOP! TURN AROUND BEFORE IT'S TOO LATE!" Two brassy young men came barreling down the road in a stylish sport car and saw the sign, with the two preachers waving their white flags. They pulled up and stopped abruptly. 'What's going on here?' one of them asked sarcastically. 'Are you two fundamentalist preachers, out here trying to save the world? Well, we don't need your help!' And with that the driver pushed the accelerator to the floor and they roared off down the road. Twenty seconds later there was the screech of tires and then a big splash. The preachers looked at each other and one said, 'Do you think we should have made a sign that simply said, BRIDGE OUT AHEAD?'

With no big warning sign or white flags, science has just passed science fiction without even stopping. Things are happening in real time now, more spectacular than in science fiction.

On May 25, 2008, the robotic spacecraft, *Phoenix,* landed on Mars to search for microbial life forms and to study the history of water there. After traveling over one hundred forty-five million miles from the earth, the spacecraft landed on a designated spot called "Green Valley," Then, one year later, the space craft, Curiosity, made a new landing on the soil of Mars. And neither was science fiction.

On March 6, 2009, the spacecraft, *Kepler,* was launched on a mission to search the Milky Way galaxy for earth-like planets. Using special telescopes, it detects dips in a star's brightness to indicate an orbiting planet is passing between the spacecraft and the star. And that isn't science fiction.

On March 3, 2009, an asteroid, the size of a ten story building, buzzed our earth, passing forty-eight thousand miles away, or about one fifth of the way to the moon. And we knew about it because scientists are now tracking objects in space. And that's not science fiction.

One hundred years earlier, an asteroid plunged into the earth in Siberia, leveling more than eight hundred square miles of forest. Many believe that it was an event like this which brought about the extinction of the dinosaurs sixty-five thousand years ago. The movie, *Jurassic Park*, is about dinosaurs and is science fiction, but that asteroid wasn't.

In 2008, the Large Hadron Collidor in Switzerland began operation as an international research project of one hundred eleven nations, to study the smallest known particles of existence. This gigantic scientific instrument will expand our understanding of the inner working of atoms, never tested before on that micro scale. Now, using that largest machine ever built, Fabriola Gianotti and her team have discovered the Higgs Boson as the smallest unit of all existence. While that may seem like science fiction, it is not.

Instruments, like these are real-time explorations and are adding to our understanding of who we are in the oneness of all molecular existence. Brought forward from Solomon's time, new insight in our time run parallel to his sense of inquiry in which he said, '*The intelligent man is always open to new ideas. In fact, he looks for them.*'

As a parallel to that, we can say, 'The intelligent church is always open to new ideas. In fact, it looks for them.' A smart church! That's what I call this church. We are beginning to talk about smart cities, smart cars and rail systems, smart energy systems, smart health programs, smart phones and computers. It's time to think about being smart churches - about flagship models that focus collective attention on a mission that brings healing and wholeness to the human story in each church's particular place in the story in the long progression of faith. And this church is leading the way. It is a flagship church on the leading edge of the future instead of the holding of the past. It represents the future toward which today's smart church can be moving.

A smart church respects the oneness of all existence as a vital center for the new sacred.

A smart church thinks about how it can be humanitarian, not just religious.

A smart church seeks a balance between worship and service.

A smart church aligns its theology with science so it advances us toward our highest humanity.

A smart church helps its people have programs which inform wise choices, promote wholesome living, and develops creative activities for its children, youth, and families.

A smart church helps its people to be world citizens on location in their time and place in the amazing human story, and in the universe where its ongoing mysterious existence is a part of our story and our story is a micro part of its story.

New knowledge. New ideas. New paradigms – the search is on as never before, and a smart church is always searching for new ideas that help people live smart lives. It's all part of the new sacred. It's about what we have inherited, but also, what we are adding to that legacy out of our place in the story. It is what helps us dream our best dreams and then give them their best chance to be the story we live out each day. That is not science fiction. That is the new sacred.

But we have a long way to go yet, in which we need to redeem tomorrow from the brokenness of yesterday, personally and as the world family.

Because "into each life some rain must fall," we all know about hurt, disappointment, the wrongs others do to us, and the wrongs we do to ourselves that leave us with regret, resentment, bitterness, even anger that can build up. We may have known the tragedies of war first hand, may have felt the impact of crime, and may have our own stories of the hurt from the brokenness of fractured relationships. That leaves us needing smart churches that generate the healing forces in which the Big Ten qualities are at the heart of our worship, learning, and service. That make us students in the school of new beginnings where we need to be sure we are working on building a better future instead of bemoaning the unchangeable failures from the past.

That makes us needing to be a church where we become a supportive healing fellowship to replace regret, anger, disgust, broken dreams and fractured relationships, with the healing words that help make us to be Big Ten people. And that is not science fiction. That is being a Big Ten Smart Church in the sunrise of new tomorrows.

As a Big Ten Smart Church, leading the way to sunrise tomorrows, we can be focused on three things. One, respect for our molecular oneness. Two, our planet home. Three, an overarching umbrella of faith.

RESPECT FOR OUR MOLECULAR ONENESS

What we have been looking for in civilization's long progressive story, and what we are looking for when we are sending space craft into the distant places in cosmic space, and what we are searching for in our elementary particle accelerators is a better understanding of who we are. What we are learning about who we are is that we have a molecular existence in common with the elementary particles of all existence. We are one. And, as part of that oneness of existence, we are learning that human beings are very, very special!

As the current extension of the long progression of the earth story has extended from the age of sticks and stones, up to computers and cell phones, our story is a marvel of all existence. And as we expand our search in the universe for other life forms, we may become even more aware of just how unique our own story here on planet earth has been, really is now, and can be in the future. Even if we get to a time in the future when we can compare our story with that of other civilizations on other planets, or if we learn when alien visitors arrive here on this planet, our story and its progression up to this wonderful time in history is a marvel of all existence and should be highly respected.

Yes, progress in our story has been slower than we wish it could have been. We have had far to many disappointments and failures.

Even so, it is a remarkable story! And now, what we can do to give our greatest respect for the journey we have come over, is to dream of an even greater future which is now entrusted into our care.

We are one family on this little planet. We have a common heritage and a common destiny with the molecular activity of the universe and may not go on forever. Everything is a part of everything else. In cosmic time, everything will change and become a part of something else, part of intergalactic events taking place in our solar system, in the Milky Way Galaxy, in millions of other galaxies, and in an endless universe. Our story doesn't have to go on forever for it to be very important and special, and be lived out with great respect as a new sacred. It's here on our mysterious journey that, *'The intelligent man is always open to new ideas. In fact, he looks for them.'*

In our age of inquiry, with new tools for exploration, micro and macro, We are learning more about how things work, and how we can work with how things work. As all this goes on, we are seeking a faith that uses what we are learning to help us define who we are, and what part we can play to live a wise and successful life in our time in history. With Moses of old, we stand on holy ground, and must take off our shoes in respect and awe as we explore the new burning bush of the wonders of existence and the new sacred.

So, can we be optimistic about the future? Yes. And why? It's because the future we ask for is leading us to cross a great divide to a new paradigm where we are building a new partnership of science and faith, woven together by the humanitarian qualities of the Big Ten Universal Qualities.

When these qualities guide our best dream we will have gone beyond the sunset paradigms of yesterday and are awakening to the sunrise paradigms new tomorrows as the new sacred. In the dawning light of a knowledge-based faith we can have great hope for our future because we will be building the better side of our humanity as our place in the story.

A place in the story - that's all any of us ever get, but that is no small place!

As I bring my delightful time here to a close, I am deeply indebted to all of you, and especially to Tim Minton. He has opened new possibilities for the book I am in the process of writing. Tim has been recording each of our sessions, so that as he puts it, others can listen in on our time together.

So, with adaptations and editorial changes, I have decided that these very special sessions we have shared together will be my book. And, in a deep gratitude to all of you, the book is hereby dedicated to the people of Center Church. You helped write, *A Place in the Story*.

SEQUELS: New Tomorrows, Apple Blossom Time, The Future We Ask For, A Place In The Story, Eagles View Mountain, Sunrise Dreams, The New Sacred.